Chances Are

Trish Dulka

BookReality

***

To Daddy

Sorry it took so long.

Morning Line

Horse racing seems made for the movies. Its most prominent stars are the horses: from those precious first moments after birth when they miraculously find the strength and coordination to raise themselves up on those four skinny, wobbling legs to the moment they charge out of a starting gate, running their hearts out for the entertainment and enrichment (or impoverishment) of humans in the stands.

Some horses run because it's in their blood and they genuinely want to. Others run simply because the little guy on their back is pounding the crap out of them with that damn leather stick. But the cameras love those big brown eyes, flowing manes, and graceful, nervous prancing, and—if you watch carefully enough—you'll notice the horses seem to love the camera, too. Many thrive and flourish on the attention of doting grooms and trainers and throngs of adoring fans. Next time you're at a track, pay special attention during the post-parade to find the horse eyeing the crowd of humans up: that's the one you want to put your money on because he's confident enough to look humans in the eye. He's looking to see if you're worthy of seeing his awesomeness in action.

Horse racing co-stars a cast of colorful human characters that even fiction writers would have a hard time making up:

- The trainers: wise and clever chess players who try to figure out the best plan to win enough money for the owner to afford the trainer's bills without running the horse to death.
- The owners: those few folks with so much money they decide to throw some away on "the sport of kings" to prove to the world they're rich enough to do so.
- The grooms: dedicated workers taking care of their charges from dawn to dinner every damn day of the week. No one knows those horses better than the grooms. They know if their horses will run well that day by how the horse looks at them that morning. They know it by how the horse kicks at the stall wall—or them. They know it by the smell of the horse's farts after their breakfast grain. So here's another little insider tip; if you ever want to make money betting at the races, befriend the grooms.

But big-time Hollywood scripts rarely focus on those behind-the-scenes workers.

The characters who usually steal the show at the horse races are the jockeys, those colorfully clad, petite-but-mighty men and women who bravely sit on the backs of the thousand-pound steeds running at nearly forty miles per hour for up to a mile and a half, balancing on two little metal rings while holding two little leather strings.

What could possibly go wrong—right?

When these riders aren't racing, they're working out to maintain the strength needed to do what they do for up to eight races every day, or they're scrounging around trying to get more mounts for the next day's races, or they're throwing up their breakfast so they make the weight assigned to them for the big race later that day. And when it comes to race time, if the horse wins, it's the horse's heart that got them there. When a horse loses, it's always the jockey's fault.

And then there is the supporting cast.

Many other people in racing help produce the daily magic: from the crew working the starting gate that has to get the high-strung, stoked-up horses into their metal cells and calm them down long enough to bang the gates open and launch them into the task at hand; to the track officials organizing the races and watching to make sure the rules aren't broken; to the thousands of people who come to watch and gamble and cheer the pretty horses as they thunder down the track to get their nose under that thin little finish wire first; to the spouses of those grooms and trainers and jockeys who have to wonder each night if their loved one is coming home with a paycheck, or with a broken arm, or if they're coming home at all, just to leave them again in a few hours in the dark of the next morning.

Cut to a grim, dimly lit office in the track's business building. The track's oddsmaker (yes, that's a real job) sits at a putty colored metal desk working on the morning line odds—calculating how a horse will probably run that day—for tomorrow's racing program. This person spends hours reviewing past performance statistics, numbers, and even old-fashioned film reels. They compare and contrast those numbers ad nauseam. They check the performance records of trainers and riders and the winning percentages of trainer/owner combinations. They'll compare how a horse last ran on a fast dry track, a firm turf track, or a sloppy, rain-soaked dirt track. Essentially, the oddsmaker is re-searching a horse's chances of winning each race they run in. Ha. Good luck with that, buster. Chance is a bitch.

But, as we all know, not every story can be a picture-perfect movie with beautiful stars and starlets with shiny white teeth and sparkles in their well-lit eyes. Real life has too many flawed characters with broken plot lines and predictable endings. If we're being honest, most stories in horse racing are simply about people trying to make a living doing what they love doing. Some were born into it, some chose to enter it, and some balance precariously between the two. This story starts at Kensington Downs, outside Cincinnati, on an otherwise-typical early summer morning.

Backside

Gennie sensed the car stalking her from the moment she walked into the track parking lot. It was easy to hear the tires crunch on the crappy, broken asphalt in the early morning silence. The lot was nearly empty since it was only 4:30 a.m., and it was still dark, real dark, with the only light coming from the widely placed parking light poles. And here she was: a sixteen-year-old girl, alone in a dark, deserted parking lot, with a car following her. She walked this way every day to get to her job as a stable hand for one of Kensington Park's top trainers, and she could probably walk it with her eyes closed if she needed to. But now was not the time. She decided to pick up the pace and try to cut across the vast lot to get onto the sidewalk where she could make a beeline for the stables if she had to.

The car sped up and met her pace. The driver's electric window rolled down, and she heard a male voice say, "Excuse me?"

She wasn't sure if most rapists or murderers were polite, but she was, so she turned to try to make eye contact and respond. "Yes?" she said as she kept walking at a crisp pace, just in case. The car (now she could see it was a newer, pretty decent Jeep) kept moving at the same speed. She couldn't see much in the dark but could tell the driver was a young guy—maybe her age, maybe a little older—and he didn't give a sketchy vibe at all. Her shoulders relaxed but her brain remained on high alert, and her hand remained tight on her phone.

"Could you tell me where employees are supposed to park?" he asked, with his elbow leaning out the window.

"But you're not an employee," she stated matter-of-factly.

"I am starting today," he said.

"Who hired you?" Gennie asked as she peeked back at him, trying not to trip over anything while briskly walking. Was she afraid of falling and becoming easy prey to this predator, or simply scared of embarrassing herself in front of the new guy?

"OK, so you must be in charge of track security?" he asked with a grin she caught on one of her peeks.

The darkness hid her blushing but she kept her head down, looking at her boots so she wouldn't see his grin again. "I'm sorry. It's none of my business. Employees park over there, to the right." She pointed to the reserved area and kept walking.

He pulled his car up, still keeping pace with her steps. "Mr. Wayne is letting me do some workouts. My uncle's a trainer. They worked together a few years back."

Rob was Gennie's boss, too. He hadn't mentioned a new hire.

"Why don't you work for your uncle?" Gennie asked, thinking she had never had a guy follow her in a car before.

"He decided to move out west. I've been working his horses since I was twelve, though. Do I pass the test? Can I come in now?" He grinned, and she couldn't help but smile back.

"If you couldn't, I wouldn't have told you where to park," she said as she finally reached and stepped up to the sidewalk to the stables so he couldn't follow her anymore. She heard the Jeep's tires crunch away, so she could tell he was driving to the employee parking area. She wondered if he had been flirting— or was she?

Rob officially introduced them later that morning as he gave the new kid a tour of the track grounds and came across Gennie and her dad, Hank, reading the day's program in the stands before the crowds started pouring in.

"Hey guys, this here is Pat Southgate, the nephew of a friend of mine in Kentucky. He's training to be a rider, and he's doing some exercising for me," Rob said. "Pat, these two can teach you everything you need to know about racing and Kensington. This is Hank Harrison, one of the top riders here for about ten years now. Always at or near the top of the leaderboards. And this is his daughter, Gennie. You'll see her in the barns, too. She's my star stable hand—when she's not too busy with school, anyway." Rob gave her a friendly wink.

Pat extended his hand first to Hank, then to Gennie, each time saying, "Nice to meet you," with a hint of a southern accent. Gennie had been correct that morning that he had dark hair and now, in the sunshine, she could see he also had brown eyes. A movie effect might have had them sparkle at this moment.

Hank eyed the newcomer with concern—obviously just another kid that would steal his morning mounts—but shook his hand anyway. Gennie grinned with embarrassment as she shook his hand. "I'm sorry if I was rude this morning," she said. "We just don't get many new people around here." Did his handshake with Gennie last just a little longer than it had with Hank? Perhaps.

Pat shrugged and smiled his effortless, contagious smile at her as Hank quickly led Gennie away by the elbow, saying they had to get to lunch. His paternal radar realized immediately that the new kid might be stealing more than just his morning rides.

And he was right.

Within days, Pat and Gennie became friends, and within weeks they were inseparable. She watched his transformation from exercise rider to race rider, and she was there to cheer his first victory and to help nurse his first fall. He provided a comforting ear when she needed to vent about her parents' declining marriage or the lame kids at her school. He had finished high school on an accelerated program back in Louisville (his parents' only requirement before they would let him leave their house), and he could frequently help her with her homework. Pat became Gennie's best friend in a life full mostly of older, cigar-smoking men. "Pat and Gennie" was more frequently said by people at the track than either name alone. Pat and Gennie were solidly connected, and everyone knew it. Pat and Gennie seemed to be the real stars of the Kensington show.

Love and Marriage

But hold up: what brought us to this particular place with these characters? Let's take a moment to watch the flashback reel that explains what brought Mr. Hank Harrison, once a promising young rider with all the skill needed to make it to horse racing's big time, to a small, mid-America track with much less potential.

As with most interesting stories, there was a beautiful woman involved.

Sylvia Honeychurch had a privileged upbringing thanks to her daddy's national chain of restaurants, but, like most fairy-tales, her mother died when Sylvia was just a kid. It turns out even big money can't always fix rare heart conditions when they're discovered too late. Daddy spared no expense to ease his depression over his wife's death by accommodating his only child's love of horses. The handsome and wealthy widower never remarried, despite the flirtations of many gold-digging women around him. Instead, he focused on keeping his wife's memory alive within their beloved little daughter. Sylvia got the best horses he could buy and the best riding lessons from the top local professionals. Sylvia competed in show jumping and had aspirations of making the Olympic team when, at the tender age of eighteen, she met Hank Harrison at an event at the Kentucky Horse Park. The foster home survivor won her over with his rags-to-riches story, his crystal blue eyes and warm smile, his kiddish enthusiasm for horses (just like her!), and his constant crooning of Sinatra standards. He could find a song for any occasion. "You Make Me Feel So Young" on his birthday. "The Way You Look Tonight" on a romantic dinner date. "I've Got You Under My Skin" when he got a rash. Suddenly, all of Sylvia's ambitions got rerouted into following her new boyfriend's racing schedule instead of her competition circuit.

Sylvia's father was furious that his daughter threw away all the years of training and competing (and all the money he had spent on making that happen) for a "loser older man from the sticks" and threatened her the only way he knew how: to disown her from himself and the family fortune. It seemed crazy now to think that Sylvia was so in love with Hank at that point in her life that she chose him over money, but it must have been the case. Gennie was born earlier than expected, which sealed the family deal: Grandpa was never heard from again. Gennie only knew him by the TV commercials he made as spokesman for the restaurants—cheesy spots of him biting into giant burgers and smiling. A smile she had never seen in person. A grandpa who had never taken her fishing or to a ballgame or for a ride on the riding lawn mower—or whatever grandpas were supposed to do with their grandkids. Gennie didn't know.

You can't miss what you never had. As a little girl, Gennie's whole world was just her parents, and she felt like the belle of the ball.

As the saying goes, behind every successful man is a woman. And Hank was indeed successful back then. Sylvia often took the credit for finding him the best opportunities by spotting a good mount when she saw it.

The scratchy home movies of the 1990s show a happy nuclear family in the winner's circle. In every shot, Hank Harrison, the handsome and young leading midwestern jockey, was aboard another stakes-winning colt, with the colt's owner and trainer on one side and Hank's beautiful wife holding hands with an adorable little pig-tailed Gennie on the other side. The same scene played over in multiple cities: Chicago, Louisville, Saint Louis, Cincinnati, Des Moines … Shiny, happy people.

But over the years, Sylvia tired of the travel and wanted to stay in one place to develop the connections that well-heeled women want to make. How can you schedule coffee dates when you don't know what date you'll be in town?

So they settled.

Hank became a regular rider at Kensington Downs outside of Cincinnati. Things started out pretty good. He topped the leading rider boards for the whole last half of the 1990s, and Sylvia got to wine and dine with the wives of other owners and trainers.

Then the wins started slowing down.

It wasn't really concerning at first—a slip down to second, then third, on the leaderboard happens to the best of them. But then Hank went a whole week without a single win. Then a month. He went from being the kid who could talk any mount into winning, to the pretty reliable guy, to the rider who was usually available, to the jock begging for jobs who was willing to take a reduction in the riding fee if it got him the gig.

Not good, not professional, and definitely not what Sylvia had envisioned for her future.

Sylvia started to notice a slowdown in her social invitations. There were suddenly fewer returned calls when she'd extend invitations. Then Hank told her they'd have to downsize from their suburban home with a circular driveway and outdoor water feature to an apartment closer to the track, so he could walk to work because, well, they only had one car now since he sold his to one of Rob's grooms.

It took less than two decades for Sylvia to start understanding what Daddy had been trying to tell her. It turns out money can buy happiness. Well, to be fair, maybe it's more like lack of money can't buy happiness. Sylvia's coveted climb of the Cincinnati horse racing social ladder turned out to be more of a stepping stool, and even that got kicked away from under her. She was bored, frustrated, and hungry for the life she once had.

Our pretty socialite felt like she was losing her sparkle. She found herself living a Cinderella story in reverse. It seemed she used all the magic fairy dust on a happy beginning instead of a happy ending. Her prince turned out to be a pauper. Her castle turned into a four-unit apartment building shared with single parents and old geezers who hadn't planned well for retirement. Her gowns were gathering dust in a box that had yet to be unpacked. There hadn't been "happy" in her "ever after" for a few years now.

Some mothers would throw themselves into protecting their offspring and ensuring they were cared for and protected from life's harsh lessons. They would avoid their worldly woes by snuggling with their babies and making them feel like royalty. They would realize their most prized possession was something that didn't come with a receipt.

But Sylvia was the other type of mother, the type that needed to take care of herself first and foremost before she could care for anything else. Like the flight attendants say, "Parents, put on your oxygen mask first before assisting children." Sylvia put on her oxygen mask but then sat back to reflect on what was causing this pressure loss instead of assisting poor little Gennie.

Luckily, even by that age, Gennie knew to grab that mask and adjust the airflow to save herself. She was Hank's daughter, you see.

Sylvia was finally seeing what Daddy had tried to tell her when she had been too young, too naive, and too stubborn to listen.

She hated being wrong.

But she hated not having privilege more.

Our little socialite started taking those socializing skills outside the home when Gennie and Hank were at the track. Sylvia began visiting places where she got noticed—where people showered her with attention and adoration and where she could win some money to buy her new things that her husband wouldn't allow anymore. Sylvia became the star of Ohio's gambling casinos by day. She didn't realize that she was just one of many sad and lonely women who walked through those doors feeling the same way every day. Those casino employees know how to make every single woman feel like a princess who is to be adored and desired. Every woman was a queen entitled to rule a kingdom and have people wait on her every need. Every woman was to be made to feel special. Even if they definitely were not.

Bug Boy

During a jockey's first year of being a jockey, an asterisk goes next to their name in the racing program. Long ago, trackers nicknamed these novice riders "bug boys" because the asterisk looked like a squished bug next to their name in print. Those old guys love to be funny. But the Racing Association felt it was important for the betting public to know that the human steering their betting choice was less experienced than other riders, just in case they knew about how hard it is to steer a thousand pounds of speeding flesh next to several other thousands of pounds of racing flesh in tight traffic. You didn't want to be around the jocks' room after a race where a novice made an error that could have brought down another horse or rider. Yeah, novices get schooled right quick because the other riders make sure of it for their own safety.

On the day of Pat's first race—a five-horse field of fillies and mares who were at least three years old—his parents were in the audience among a crowd of regulars who were regular enough to recognize that a new name was in the program. Pat was riding Miss Sugar, one of Gennie's charges from Rob's barn. She was a docile, obedient bay filly who would do anything for a sugar cube. In the ring, Rob gave Pat the same advice he would have told any rider. He knew this kid was ready, and he wanted to treat him like a professional to make him feel more comfortable.

"Let her break the way she wants to; she usually likes to jump right to the lead. And that's fine. Move to the rail if you can. Then just try to keep her relaxed and don't let her burn out too quick. The race is only six furlongs, so she can go wire to wire if she doesn't set a pace that's too excruciating."

Pat nodded in understanding, and Rob cupped his hands to hoist Pat's bended knee up into the saddle of the steady mare. Pat's face remained calm, but those who knew him best would recognize he was pale. And if you got really close to him, you might see that his hands were grasping the reins so tight there were indents in the skin of his fingers.

Gennie was on the lead pony that took his mare out to the starting gate. After they passed out of the paddock area, full of bettors sizing up the field and little kids checking out the pretty horses, Gennie looked over to do her own review.

"You're not going to puke, are you?" she asked.

His eyes looked up though his riding helmet remained in the same downward position. "Has that ever happened in a race?"

"Nope," she replied, "and it's not going to today either. The other riders would never let you live that down, so suck it up, buttercup, and ride like a big boy. Miss Sugar is in a good mood today, and I promised her another sugar cube if she's good to you." The filly eyed up Gennie as she talked. Her ears were pointed forward, and she had a lively spring in her step.

Pat forced a slight smile but didn't speak. This was it. This was when he got to prove that skipping all those childhood invites so he could practice his gymkhana events instead was worth it. This was when he got to prove that riding was more than just a hobby. This was when he got to prove that everything he gave up to be here was for a good reason. No pressure, kid.

Once they got close to the starting gate, one of the assistant starters walked over to take the lead rope from Gennie to guide Miss Sugar into her stall. Gennie gave Pat a reassuring smile and shouted, "You got this!" Pat nodded. Gennie rode her horse over to the side of the track to watch the break with the outriders who monitored each race on horseback just in case something went wrong. Gennie knew that if Pat could get a clean break out of the gate, he should be good to go. But if he fell off at that initial charge, it would be a long walk back to the jocks' room.

As Gennie's cousin Carl and his crew loaded the rest of the horses into the starting gate, the other riders teased Pat about his first race. But all of them, even Hank, were good-natured about it. They all remembered their first races and knew the light-hearted joking might help the kid get through it.

The bell clanged, the gates banged open, and the five fillies and mares charged out.

Pat didn't fall off.

Miss Sugar did what Rob said she would: she bounded to the lead and instinctively went for the rail. Pat held on and felt he was in control. There was no one right next to him, but he could tell there were one or two right behind him. He bent his head down further to look under his arms to confirm they were behind him but not moving up. He hollered to Miss Sugar to keep steady, go easy, and oh, what a pretty girl she was. Her ears flickered back and forth, but her eyes remained straight ahead. Pat relaxed and remembered why he loved riding at full gallop: it was the closest to flying a man could get.

They made the final turn, and Miss Sugar saw the end in sight. That final straight stretch was fun. And the crowd cheering was exciting. And maybe that girl with the sugar cube was up ahead. The little guy on her back wasn't as mean as other riders she'd had. Miss Sugar put it into the next gear and surged forward.

Pat looked under his arm to see behind him and was amazed to see those other two horses further behind him than before. He hoped he wasn't pushing Miss Sugar too hard, but then realized he had forgotten to use his whip.

That nice little filly went wire to wire, and Pat would forever have bragging rights that he won the first race he rode.

Gennie knew that Rob gave him that mount because it would be an easy one. Rob was that kind of guy. But she would never tell Pat that. She knew it was better for him to believe it was all him who made the magic happen. Confidence and experience are the two primary tools for having a safe ride. Luck plays a role, too, but no man can control that, try as they might.

Gennie rode over to catch the cantering winning filly, gave Pat a high five, and reached into her pocket to give Miss Sugar not just one but a handful of sugar cubes. She looked at Pat, who was still pale but had his full-blown smile out now.

"You better wipe that grin off your face before the other riders see it. You're going to be dead to them now," she advised. She knew they were kind to newcomers until they got better than them. With Pat, that was going to start much sooner than most.

That year, Pat took Kensington by storm with the best riding record of any bug boy in recent memory. He often rode six out of eight daily races, usually winning at least one. He pulled in a pretty good salary for an eighteen-year-old. Most of the old-timers resented Pat with his hotshot record and luck. "He hasn't paid his dues," said people like Carl. "He won't be so hot when his first losing streak comes." They didn't trust a good-looking youngster who came out of nowhere to conquer their home turf. To trainers, though, Pat was a rider who could get their horses to win. He was a reliable worker who had good hands and a calm disposition. To Gennie, he was the only friend under thirty years old she had.

Lady Luck Takes a Leave of Absence

After nearly a year of Hank's dismal winning record, only the oldest trainers gave him work for a small fee. Those guys wouldn't abandon a fellow old-timer when his luck was off. They knew that Lady Luck takes turns with people in horse racing, and if you didn't help the guy at the bottom, your turn could be next. But most of the younger owners and trainers paid more attention to statistics than superstition. Most of the cocky younger riders were quick to tell Hank his days were numbered. Pat, of course, was not among those guys. He tried to help Hank when he could, referring trainers to him when Pat wasn't available to take an offered mount. Pat's efforts were usually in vain. But at least he tried.

Gennie spent every day at the races trying to be her dad's biggest cheerleader or, more accurately, often his only cheerleader. On this particular gloomy early spring day, Gennie wasn't feeling it.

What's it going to be this time, Dad? Second by a nose? Last by a mile? Or fifth place—just one spot away from bringing in a share of the purse? She hated when her thoughts went to dark places as she watched her father ride, despite her best mental attempts to remain positive. She noticed that she had to have these internal battles more often in recent days.

"Here they come!" A little girl wearing a pink "I love horses" T-shirt was next to Gennie, jumping up and down and clapping and hollering with delight as she watched the horses race into the home stretch. Gennie momentarily looked away from the horses to smile at the girl's excitement and wonder if she had ever been so young. Gennie closed her eyes to capture the mental snapshot of the excited youngster and made a silent vow to keep optimistic about Hank's career.

But the crowd's intensifying roar made her turn her attention back to the track. The first three horses raced neck and neck for the finish line. Their jockeys were shouting, standing in their stirrups with their arms pumping to encourage—or threaten—their horses to get to that wire first. The three leaders crossed under it within noses of each other. The bright orange PHOTO FINISH letters lit up the jumbotron, and the crowd groaned in unified impatience.

While most of the crowd quickly turned from the rail to debate with their companions who won, or to go to the paddock to check out the next race's entries, or to grab a beer at the concession stand, Gennie stayed watching the track from the side rail. She was the still and silent black-and-white actress in sharp focus in an art film, surrounded by swirling blurred colors and a cacophony of noise. She waited for the race's sixth and final horse and his jockey to finally cross the finish line, twelve long lengths behind those three motivated leaders. She sighed loudly and finally looked away.

It was the seventh race of the day and another humiliating loss for her dad.

The little girl in pink who had brought her a momentary smile was gone, as was Gennie's new pledge to herself. So much for remaining positive.

She decided to go home early.

She walked through the ticket-littered grandstand past the hundreds of strangers whose eyes were locked on the monitors replaying the finish in slow motion. She kept her head low and her eyes on her weathered riding boots as they crossed the stained floors into the public paddock area. Grooms were already walking the horses for the next race around and around the big, shaded circle, whispering gently to their high-strung charges to keep them calm. A few serious gamblers were there, astutely eyeing up the contenders to see who was most likely to defy big odds and earn them some rent money.

Gennie dipped under the crossing gate to walk right through the paddock, careful not to make eye contact with any of the grooms in the ring. It was near impossible for her to walk anywhere on the Kensington grounds without knowing someone. But she didn't feel like talking today. Instead, she had to think of ways to help Hank get out of his slump.

Despite her best efforts to be unseen, she heard someone say, "Over a hundred now?"

She nodded her glum acknowledgment to the trainer and kept walking. Damn it. Of course, they were keeping track of Hank's losses, probably in a betting pool among employees. How many races would Hank go without a win? Damn, someone was going to win a lot of money one day. But what day?

Once beyond the paddock stalls, Gennie had a clear shot from the parking lot to the walkway that led her through the rows of stables. She nodded to the security gate worker, keeping her head down so he wouldn't notice the rare tear running down her cheek, and crossed over to the public sidewalk for the final blocks leading to their apartment building.

Once safely beyond the track grounds, she started to think of how to avoid her mom when she got home. Sylvia would no doubt pounce on her for news of the day: did Hank win any?

Did he at least place in any races, so they might get a little bonus? Did he fall and die so she could at least cash in the life insurance policy?

Sylvia was not the kindest of women. And today, Gennie just wasn't in the mood to tolerate her.

Gennie knew Sylvia would be all over her as soon as she opened the door. Then, when she'd hear it was just another day of losses, she'd go back to watching her soap operas or court TV or QVC, or painting her nails, or whatever the hell she did all day while Hank and Gennie were at the track working. She wouldn't ask Gennie how her day was, how she was holding up, or if she wanted a snack before dinner. Gennie was pretty sure Sylvia longed for money so that she could have hired nannies to do the work she was supposed to. Instead, she let most of the parenting responsibilities fall on Hank. He wasn't great at it either, but when Gennie thought back to late-night homework sessions or parent-teacher conferences, it was always Hank who was by her side.

Gennie had learned quickly to be independent of her parents. By the time she was twelve, she was hanging out in the track's backstretch, picking up stable work from any of the trainers who had watched her grow up and treated her like their own family. If she wasn't at the track, she was in her room, avoiding her parents' constant arguments by reading racing magazines or watching national races on TV.

This afternoon could have been a scene from one of Sylvia's soap operas.

The first thing Gennie noticed when she opened the apartment door was the silence that greeted her. Their apartment was never void of the noise of the TV her mom usually had blaring. Not only was there no TV noise, but there was also no hollering from Sylvia asking how the hell Hank did today. Just silence: surprising, peaceful silence.

The second thing Gennie noticed was the note hanging dramatically from the hall ceiling light with wrapping paper ribbon. She should have made a noose for it, Gennie thought as she tore it down. Gennie held the note in her hands and looked around the living room, trying to decide what to do next. Her eyes stopped on the old, rusted horseshoe carefully mounted on the wall, facing upward, to hold in good luck for the family. She sighed out loud for the second time that afternoon as her head spun with options. She almost didn't open the note. She knew what it would say. But she knew she would have to read the actual words to tell Hank.

Gennie opened the carefully folded note. It was in Sylvia's handwriting, unusually elegant for someone who always seemed so frantic and anxious. Sylvia wrote about the things she usually complained about: Hank's lack of ambition; Hank's inability to understand her needs and, heaven forbid, ever try to meet them; Hank's inevitable contentment regardless of their income; etc. And Bruce. She raved about Bruce, her new boyfriend. Bruce was a guy Sylvia had met at the Indian casino and had made no secret about it from the start. According to the note, Bruce was energetic, resourceful, and exciting. Gennie had hoped Sylvia was using Bruce to make Hank understand she could leave him if things didn't improve. In fact, Gennie thought Bruce was fictitious, a fantasy Sylvia invented to taunt Hank. But Gennie must have been wrong—he was real. This was really happening.

Sylvia wrote that she realized the racetrack life wasn't for her anymore, but she knew that both Hank and Gennie would never consider leaving it.

She got one thing right, Gennie thought. And at least she put this in writing instead of trying to have a "family conference", as she would call them. That would have just led to another match of Mom screaming, Dad ignoring her, and Gennie slamming her bedroom door.

At the end of the note, Sylvia announced that she was moving to St. Louis and would be in touch.

Be in touch.

What kind of mom says that?

Gennie felt her hands shaking as she finished the letter. It took all her energy not to rip the paper to shreds. She wanted to scream obscenities and smash something. But she didn't. Instead, she made a tight-lipped smile, looked around the quiet room, and realized that things might actually be better now. Maybe their luck was changing.

It could have been much worse. What if Sylvia had expected Gennie to come with her? Eww. Gennie would never set foot in a room with Bruce. No freaking way. So Sylvia was leaving to start a new life, a better life—on her own with Bruce, ignoring her marital vows and leaving behind her only child.

Gennie let out a deep, slow breath to calm her pounding heart and set the note on the kitchen table. Should she feel worse about her mom, the woman who gave her life, being gone? Why the hell should she when the woman signed her note that she'd "be in touch"? But Sylvia was at least humane enough to realize that it was better for Gennie to stay here because, after all, Hank would need someone to take care of him. So, Gennie thought, maybe that was evidence that despite the years of fighting and disappointment, perhaps deep down Sylvia did still care for Hank. Or maybe she just realized that if she asked Gennie to choose where she'd rather be, she knew, without a doubt, Gennie would never choose her mother over the track.

But damn her for breaking Hank's heart. Gennie's fist hit the kitchen table, surprising her. Damn her! Hank might not be the most expressive guy in the world, but Gennie knew that he loved Sylvia with every ounce of his small but muscular body, and he was proud to call her his wife. He always said she made him feel like a million bucks, and she always replied, "Then show me the money." Of course, he would never admit it, but this would hurt him much more than the losing streak. Gennie knew he didn't show much emotion over losing, which drove Sylvia crazy, but she wasn't sure how he would handle this. All she knew was that she was much more worried about how Hank would handle this loss than how it would affect her. Maybe Gennie should have done more to get those two to communicate better. She had had a ringside seat for hundreds of arguments and misunderstandings over the years. Maybe she should have intervened and suggested … But wait a minute. She was the kid here. No. This was all Sylvia's fault. Gennie shook those thoughts off and went to the fridge to get a Coke. She usually could open a can with one hand—a skill Hank had taught her—but today she had to use both trembling hands to open it.

Gennie had been angry with Sylvia for a long time. She had no idea if every teenager felt the same way about their mothers—she knew Pat got along fine with his mom, but she didn't have any other teen friends at the track to ask—but Gennie knew she didn't like how her mother always picked on Hank and bothered him nonstop when he was home. All Sylvia did was complain. Gennie had difficulty remembering the last traditional mother-daughter moment they might have had. She remembered riding a Shetland pony when she was real little while her mom rode ahead of them on a beautiful big bay hunter. Mom had said the bay had won her a championship some years before. Gennie remembered looking up at her mom and thinking she was the most beautiful woman in the world. That was a long, long time ago.

Gennie took a long, hot shower with her mind racing and changed into her evening jeans, the only ones without a hole anywhere. She pulled her long brown hair back into a simple ponytail, washed her face—that face that looked like photos of her mother as a kid—clear of stable dust and grime, and went back to the track to find Hank. All the while, she practiced telling him that Sylvia was gone and that they were on their own.

Out of the Money Again

"Dad, Sylvia's gone." Gennie had practiced the words a hundred times, walking to the barns where she knew she'd find him scavenging for mounts.

"What do you mean, honey? Where'd she go?"

"Hank, she left town," Gennie's older cousin Carl clarified. Gennie enlisted Carl to help her break it to him. Gennie wasn't sure how Hank would react, and she thought—just in case his reaction was more physical or angry than she expected—it might be good to have Carl on hand to help contain him. Gennie had never seen Hank go berserk, but if ever there was a time he'd be justified in doing so, here it was. She knew she felt like throwing that damn horseshoe into the TV when she first read the note, so she figured Hank would be at least that pissed.

Hank's gray-blue eyes searched the air in front of him for clues. His forehead wrinkled a bit more.

"Dad, she just … you know, she just wasn't happy. I guess that Bruce guy is real, and they're moving to St. Louis. But, Dad, it's OK. We'll be OK." Gennie, the now seventeen-year-old baby of the family, assured her father.

Hank took the news of his wife's abandonment like the man he was: stoic and silent.

You see, a man like Hank can't let the outside world know what he's going through. His acting skills were worthy of an Oscar. Through good times and bad times, to the bitchy selfish wife or the perfectly amazing daughter, or any anxious trainer, he always stayed the same: cool, calm, collected—you had to be to be a rider. Your career was dead if a trainer saw you as volatile and unpredictable. If you're not calm under pressure when you're steering a ton of charging horse flesh worth thousands of dollars, you better find another line of work, buddy.

But Gennie and Carl both saw those aging somber gray eyes turn a little darker with the news. His fingers intertwined each other a little more quickly. And his lips got just a little tighter.

"Well," he finally said. "So that's that."

Life had thrown Hank a lot of challenges in his forty-plus years. Sylvia had been his support through most of them. He had always considered himself the luckiest man in the world for having her fall in love with him. But now it appeared that luck could be as temporary as racing luck.

At least he still had his filly, Gennie. He was still man enough to take care of his kid. She needed him to remain strong and to provide for her. And so he would. That was the only win that mattered.

So although in his mind he was throwing a tantrum—throwing hay bales into stable aisles, punching holes into barn walls (and into that fucking Bruce's face), screaming obscenities to the heavens above—to everyone else watching him, he remained quiet, calm, and in control. He had to. He had to stay strong for Gennie.

"Why don't we all go to the diner for dinner then," Hank said. "I guess we'll need to get dinner." He started heading toward the track diner. Carl and Gennie exchanged glances, and both shrugged at the same time. Carl put a reassuring arm around Gennie, and they followed in Hank's footsteps. Anyone familiar with Sinatra would recognize that the song Hank was quietly humming on the way over was, "I'll Only Miss Her When I Think of Her".

And so started the new scene of the Harrisons' life script. One less character to have to develop: the other characters forced to grow in ways they hadn't seen coming. Funny how life knows how to throw in plot twists better than the best scriptwriters in Hollywood. Funny how life likes to mess things up, shuffle things up, and then toss them on the ground to see where they'll all land, just like a seasoned gambler. Yeah, that's the secret that most people don't know: Life is just one big game of chance ... one you don't have a choice about making. Sometimes it doesn't cost you anything, and sometimes it does.

Going the Distance

"The track is no place for a girl to grow up," Hank said as he dug around in a box on the floor of their new, one-bedroom apartment at the back of Kensington Downs. He grimaced as he tried to stand straight up with a newspaper-wrapped bundle.

"The track is no place for a man to grow old," Gennie replied, four months and a hundred more losses since her mother had left.

"But we all live so close together now," intercepted Carl. "We'll all be here for each other now." Carl was the official starter at Kensington. He was the one who supervised the guys who pushed, pulled, and otherwise prodded the horses into the stalls to begin each race and then waited for the one split second every horse was finally perfectly still to push the button that banged the front gate open. He was thirty years old, with a weathered face, big hands, and a body that had long ago outgrown his dreams of being a race rider like his uncle. Carl had even lived with the Harrisons sometimes when his luck was down, and he needed to earn a few more bucks to pay his rent. That was another thing Sylvia used to complain about before she left. But Gennie always liked having him around; he was the sibling her parents had never given her. And now he was also their neighbor just down the hall.

"He's right," Gennie said, "we're one big happy family now." Hank and Gennie were moving into the backlot apartments for track employees. This new set for their family drama certainly wasn't a move-up. Migrant farm workers often had better living conditions. But when a jockey loses consistently for an entire year, the riding gigs come less frequently; the good mounts never come, and a jockey is lucky to see any purse money at all. An apartment on the backlot was the only type a single, down-on-his-luck jockey with a kid could afford.

The apartment had a small living room, an even smaller bedroom, and a nook with a sink and two-burner stovetop that a real estate agent would be hard-pressed to describe as a kitchenette. Above the small sink was a window overlooking the parking lot with barns in the distance. A yellowed lace curtain tried to filter the view. The living room could hold their couch, one old recliner, and a coffee table with a twenty-inch TV. Hank and Gennie sold the furniture from their old apartment that couldn't fit into the new one at an informal rummage sale in the track parking lot to other track employees whose luck enabled them to live off the grounds in nicer places. Gennie had used some of the rummage sale money to buy scented candles to mask the new place's lingering odor with no detectable source.

Hank stepped over the empty boxes strewn about the floor to hammer two little nails into the wall. He went back to the newspaper-wrapped package to unwrap it to reveal his lucky horseshoe. He carefully mounted it on the nails, open side up, to hold in any good luck that might happen to be in the vicinity.

Gennie and Carl stopped momentarily to watch Hank mount the tiny decoration on the otherwise empty wall. Gennie noted how Hank didn't even have to measure before pounding in the nails. Hank turned around to see why the room was suddenly silent.

"OK, guys, I better head out," Carl said as he quickly flattened the last of the moving boxes and stacked it with the empty frozen pizza boxes from their dinner. It was nine o'clock.

"Thanks for all your help, Carl," Gennie said while ringing out a rag after wiping down the last of the painted woodwork.

Hank crumbled the last ball of packing newspaper into the trash can. "You're right," he said. "That was a good day's work. Thanks, Carl. Yep, time for bed. I think we all deserve a good night's sleep."

Hank always said that like sleep was the main luxury he worked for each day.

"Yep, we sure do," Carl agreed. "See y'all tomorrow. Good night."

"Sounds good," Gennie said, closing and locking the door behind him. She turned and surveyed the new room, which finally looked more like an actual living room and less like a company mail room. "OK, Dad, nice job today. I'll see you in the morning. 'Night."

Nine o'clock was standard bedtime for the Harrisons since they were both out the door by 5:00 a.m. Hank would hit the barns to search for riding gigs. Gennie would head over to Rob's part of the track stables to tend to a handful of his horses. Since Sylvia had left and summer vacation started, Gennie became an official tracker, working full time as a groom for Rob. Although Rob admired the Harrison family, he could no longer hire Hank to ride for him. Although Rob would have loved to help Hank out, he had to put his horses and their owners' expectations above his old, soft heart. Hank just couldn't get the job done anymore, but his daughter, Gennie, was a gem. She could work for him as much as she wanted to.

Hank decided that he would sleep on the couch, and Gennie would have the bedroom. That was one decision that Gennie didn't fight. The small room only had space for her bed and dresser. The walls were the same off-white as the living room. There was one window facing the stables. The gouges on the windowsill showed many layers of paint, like the rings inside a tree. The only decoration in the room was her bulletin board with photos and newspaper clippings that she hung next to her bed so she could look at it as she tried to fall asleep at night. There was an eight-by-ten photo of her dad in the winner's circle after a stakes race with Sylvia next to him, holding his hand while he was still on the horse. Sylvia looked so young, so happy. There was a picture of Gennie as a toddler on a small brown-and-white Shetland pony that Rob had brought in as a stablemate for a stakes horse he was training at the time. There were newspaper clippings about the past three Kentucky Derby winners and an official finish line black-and-white photo of her dad's horse edging out another in the Arkansas Derby. But most of the board's space was filled up with pictures and newspaper clippings of Pat.

Looking at the photos on that old splitting-apart bulletin board was the most calming way Gennie could slow her racing mind at night when her real-world panic about money and survival and long-term dreams would keep her awake. Remembering the past good times and Pat in the present would usually relax her brain into knowing things would be OK. Tonight she couldn't help but zoom in on Sylvia's face in that old picture. That face that hadn't been seen in months. She hadn't even called. Or texted. She was just totally gone. Gennie felt her pulse quicken. She took a few deep breaths and tried to shift her focus to Pat. To her dad. To Carl. She kept telling herself she had all the family she needed long into the night.

Working the Filly

As usual, Gennie's eyes opened just before the alarm went off. She leaned over in the dark to intuitively hit the off button before the god-awful clanging began. Within minutes she was in her old jeans and Breeders Cup T-shirt, hair pulled back in a ponytail, and a Kensington baseball hat holding it in place. As she emerged from her room, her dad sat on the couch with one small lamp lighting his reading of yesterday's *Daily Racing Form*. "Have a good day, honey. See you in a bit," he said, barely looking up.

"You too, Daddy," she said, and she was out the door.

She walked in silence in the dark, with only crickets as the soundtrack. She nodded but didn't speak when other track workers neared. It was morning code to give everyone their space to wake up. Only the barn dogs were allowed to be in good moods that early.

A brilliant orange glow lit up the eastern sky, providing a rather artistic backdrop for the run-down stables that usually wouldn't be the subject of any artist's pallet.

As she approached Rob's portion of the barns, all the horses were already awake, with their heads looking out of their stalls toward her. "You guys get me every morning," she said, smiling as she took in the scene. Eight necks and heads, most brown, turned at the same angle, all looking at her with the same expression that said: FEED ME.

"Hang in there, buddies," she said quietly as she walked by, giving each a pat on the nose and a little smile as she worked her way to the feed bin. "I've only got two hands, but I'll get to ya."

She reviewed the workout and race list for the day, then started mixing the feed accordingly, making sure to feed the horses working out that morning first so they'd be done digesting before Rob and the rider showed up.

By the time the first round of feed was out, more people were in the barns and the noise level went up. This day there was talk radio in the background, which meant Milo had been the first groom to get in, but it could have been Mexican radio if it had been Angel or the local country station if Clay had gotten there first. Another unwritten code: the first groom in picks the day's soundtrack. Or, really, it was the first groom in after Gennie since she was usually first but didn't care what station was playing, so she let the guys deal with it.

The smell of coffee soon took over as the primary scent in the barn as coffee pots in tack rooms brewed fresh cups of starter fuel for the workers. Milo handed Gennie a cup of black coffee—no time or space to mess with creamers or sugar in the tack room—and each nodded silently to the other as "thanks" and "no problem". The morning crew had a complete lexicon of silent motions that they all understood.

The sound of Rob whistling some unknown melody announced his arrival. He was the only one allowed to be loud and cheerful that early, along with his Golden Retriever, Jack. "Hey, Gen, how's the herd looking today?" he asked, travel mug in one hand with a *Daily Racing Form* tucked under the other arm.

"Looking good, boss," she said while bending down to give her daily greeting to the dog, who wagged his tail and leaned his whole body against Gennie for maximum petting possibilities. "Everyone took their feed just fine."

"Good, good," Rob said. "Gonna be another hot one. Let's get the ones working this morning out as early as possible."

"You got it," Gennie said, "as long as you can get those no-good lazy riders here on time."

"Damn straight," Rob said with a grin, knowing that today's exercise riders were Hank and Pat. "Hey, I got payroll ready to distribute, so come grab your check when you're done."

"Of course," she said. Some days it still felt odd to get money for doing this. She even got bonuses each time one of "her" horses came in the money in any of their races. Gennie told everyone she worked because she loved it and that her horses needed her care in order to keep winning. But it was no secret that the Harrisons needed the money. Hank's meager riding fees barely covered their last apartment's rent. They might make it in the new place, but it still would be tight.

"Living the dream," Gennie said to herself with a smile. She took another sip of her coffee while it was still warm, and then she went back to the tack stall to start saddling up the horses.

Her Way

To the parents or legal guardians of Genuine Harrison:

This is a reminder that registration for school is on August 15. Students will receive their book lists and locker assignments, have their ID photos taken, and turn in their signed registration papers, including their immunization records. If your student needs special assistance …

The letter from PS242 sat on the Harrisons' small kitchen table. It had been picked up, read, folded, unfolded, put down, picked up, read, folded, and unfolded many times since it had arrived the day before.

The parents or legal guardians of Genuine Harrison had not yet seen it. Gennie was the one who got the mail every day, and Gennie was the one who had opened it. And refolded it. And so on. She was the one who sat in on the kitchen chair, staring at its carcass now.

It was already August 5. There was no more time to waste.

Gennie slipped on her rubber stable boots, put the letter back into its envelope and then into her back pocket, then pulled out her old, scratched flip phone to text Carl and her father:

Family meeting at diner at 6, plz?

She then started her long walk back to the backstretch.

***

"Family meeting. Sounds serious," Carl said sarcastically as he reached past Hank to get the sugar for his coffee. Hank stirred his coffee with a spoon even though he drank it black. Gennie sat across from both of them at the track diner. She had got there first to grab a table in the back corner. Although the diner was never as busy for dinner as it was for breakfast, she didn't want to take any chances. The diner's air conditioning was a relief after a long, hot day of racing. Hank's best finish was third in a field of seven. At least he brought home a little bit of a purse.

"Isn't it ironic that we're all here drinking coffee on the hottest day of the year?" Gennie started, with a slight laugh. Carl and Hank stared at her blankly.

"Believe me, if they served Long Island iced teas, I'd be drinking one of those instead," Carl responded.

Hank let out a little, "Hmph," in agreement.

Gennie watched the nearly transparent steam rise out of the depths of the cup as she began to talk. "OK, well, here goes. I've already made my decision, so I don't want to argue about it, but I want you both to know I've decided not to go back to school next month. I'm going to keep working for Rob full time, and then I'll go and get my GED at night when things slow down a bit." She cautiously raised her eyes from her cup to gauge their reactions.

Hank looked at her briefly and then went back to methodically stirring his coffee. Carl immediately sat back in his chair— his mouth open, his eyes squinting in concern—and stared at her. He shook his head as if shaking out what he really wanted to say and then started as calmly as he could, "Gennie, whoa, let's not rush into anything here. You've only got one year left. You can still work mornings and weekends. Why not just go and get it over with?"

"Because the thought of riding the bus with the stoners and the jocks and all their petty little girlfriends worrying about their big problems like what to wear to the dance just seems a little beyond me right now," Gennie said with an edge. "I think I'm a bit above hanging out with kids who think the biggest crisis in the world is not getting to use the car on Saturday night. Besides, I like my job. Why give it up to go do something I hate?"

Carl stared at her, his face growing stiff in his frustration. He leaned forward so that he wouldn't raise his voice. "You do not hate school. You're a good student. I saw your report cards. You have a lot of potential."

"It's just not my thing. Yes, getting the grades isn't the issue, which is why getting my GED will be easy. It's just all that other crap that comes with high school that I'm not into."

Carl elbowed Hank. "Aren't you going to say anything?" he asked in frustration.

Hank shrugged, avoiding eye contact. "I dropped out and did OK for myself. School's not for everyone. I learned a hell of a lot more at the track than at school."

Gennie tried to hold back a grin. She'd guessed that would be her dad's reaction—that he'd actually be proud that his little girl was following in his footsteps, however crooked and warped his own path had been. But she did feel bad about Carl. He seemed really upset with her.

Carl sighed in disappointment at Hank and Gennie, who stared back, making it clear that one stubborn mule might be hard for him to budge, but two were nearly impossible. "Gennie, OK, so you don't like school, but having a real diploma just looks so much better on a resumé than saying you've got some dumb certificate," Carl said. "You've got to think ahead, girl, and not just the way things are right here, right now. I know things are tight, but you can live without a few luxuries for a few more months."

Hank perked up. "Hey, if this is all about money, Gennie, I can add a few more workouts. Is that what this is really about? What do you need? We can work something out. If this is just about money, Gen, then don't even think about it."

Gennie straightened up and locked her steely eyes on Carl. "Luxuries? There's no such word in my vocabulary, Carl, and you know that. Dad, you just earn enough for the rent, and we'll be fine. I'm doing this because I want to, that's all." Gennie glared at Carl for bringing up the subject of money, even if that was the real reason for her decision.

Carl just shook his head. "Gennie, girl, I know you're a smart one, but I gotta tell you, I don't feel good about this. You've got a future ahead of you to think about. Do you really want to be a groom all your life? You could get a real job and make enough money to own horses if you wanted to. Or be a stable manager. Or own a racetrack! You're a smart girl. You can do more than live on a backstretch."

Gennie sat back in her chair with her arms crossed and lips tight and stared at Carl.

He knew that glare. "But I also know when there's no budging you. Hank, you work on her at home, though, OK?" Carl looked at his daydreaming uncle, who just grunted under his breath and shook his head. "Gennie, really, let's all just think about it for a while and think about maybe how to go to school and still work, OK? Maybe I'll talk to Rob—"

"Don't you dare," Gennie said. "I'm turning eighteen in a few weeks and can make my own decision about this."

Hank mumbled something as he dug in his pocket to find three crumpled-up dollars to pay for the coffee. He left the bills on the table as all three cleared out to head home for dinner. Paying for meals at the diner just wasn't in their budget.

***

The following day, after her stable duties but before the races began, Gennie found Pat in the jocks' lounge before the afternoon's first race. He was reading the *Racing Form*, ready for the races to start in his white shirt and riding pants. Sensing her as soon as she entered the room, he put the paper down. "Ping-pong?" he asked like an excited kid. Gennie was sure he'd give up riding to become a professional ping-pong player if such a profession existed. If he had the money, he would happily start the first cable channel dedicated to ping-pong games. Maybe even a reality TV show about The Wide World of Ping-Pong. Before, between, and after races, he would play the game with anyone he could find.

She smiled and shook her head as she sat down next to him. "Not today. I've got something I want to tell you."

His smile immediately disappeared. He put the paper down and looked at her carefully. He could always read her, and she hated that.

"Calm down. I'm not dying or anything," she said, but she found herself unable to meet his eyes. She looked toward the ping-pong table instead. "It's just, well, I've decided that I'm not going back to school next month. My gig with Rob is going so well that I want to keep it going. I'll get my GED at night or something. Maybe you can help me study for it."

Pat not only finished high school a year early, but he also did it with straight A's. Gennie was one of the few people at Kensington who knew that. He sensed that enough folks at Kensington already resented him for being a decent rider; he didn't need to brag about being smart, too.

Pat studied her face until she bit her lip and finally looked up to meet his stare.

"What?" she said, her voice breaking up. "Just say it. Tell me it's a stupid idea, and it's only one year, and get it over with, and you can help with money if that's the issue, blah blah blah." She felt her heart start to speed up, something that hadn't happened in her discussion with Hank and Carl.

"No, I wouldn't say that. You know that." He took her hand. "How did Hank take it?"

She laughed. "He thinks it's great that Daddy's Little Girl is following in his footsteps. Carl's not cool about it, though. I'm sure he'll be hunting me down later to try and talk me out of it. I'm afraid he's going to talk to Rob even though I told him not to. So, really, do you think I'm ruining my life? Am I destined for a life of minimum-wage, fast-food kitchen jobs?"

His eyes locked into hers again. "You wanna know what my first reaction was, really?"

She looked down again, bracing for the worst. "What?"

"I know it's not P.C., but I thought, great, we'll get to spend even more time together. I was kind of dreading the start of September."

Looking at her denim-clad knees, she smiled. "You'll help me study for that stupid test?" she asked.

"We'll make sure you pass it with flying colors," he said, squeezing her hand. She hugged him until another jock entered the lounge and made smooching noises. They both laughed, and she left him with a quick kiss and a warm smile so he could get ready for the day's first race. Suddenly, everything felt much lighter. The hot summer sun seemed less oppressive. The sky seemed bluer. And the great unknown was just a little less scary.

And thus began Gennie's life as a high school dropout. Another tick on the Ohio state statistic board about teenagers who don't get their diplomas. When school started in September, no one from her old school contacted her to ask why she wasn't there for her senior year, her senior homecoming, her senior prom, her graduation. The few kids who noticed she wasn't back assumed she had moved. Why else wouldn't she be there?

On September 3, while those kids were putting on their new clothes and piling into friends' cars to get to school, Gennie was mucking stalls, grooming handsome steeds, and unsuccessfully cheering her father on from the rail. Just another day at the track.

That's Life

Gennie and Rob watched the fifth race of the day from the rail, studying through their binoculars how the horses moved or stalled or fired. Their trained eyes could spot the subtle moves of the riders as they asked—or begged—their horses for just a little more. They could see the spark of a winner in a horse's head movements or the lost enthusiasm of a horse that would rather be anywhere else than running down this stretch. Rob's barn didn't have any horses in that race, but he was always studying horses that might come up for sale or race against his horses someday. Gennie was always studying Hank. He had a mount in this one; it was another long shot but a nice small field. Although he had an early lead, Gennie and Rob saw Hank's horse start to fade and fall back despite Hank's desperate kicks, swats, and hollers. The pounding hooves of other horses rushed by, and Hank followed them in.

Although the weather was cooling and the leaves were changing color, Hank's losing streak stayed the same. It was over 250 now.

Rob gave Gennie a fatherly pat of encouragement on the shoulder and headed back to the barn. He was already at an age when most men started thinking about retirement. He had gray hair and a friendly, weathered face from thousands of hours of standing out in the elements and watching horses run. He put his horses' needs first and treated them well, and for that, he had many winners in his stable. Owners trusted him and other trainers respected him. All the Kensington grooms aspired to work for Rob thanks to his good pay and gentle demeanor. Most trainers were as high-strung as their horses, but Rob must have come from different DNA. Most folks knew that he got his start in racing after he ran away from home and took a job as a groom at Belmont in New York, but that was the only part of his past he'd ever revealed. He once had a horse that qualified for the Kentucky Derby, but as he was preparing to leave for Louisville, the horse kicked his stall and messed up his leg. Rob had to pull him from the big race. "That's life for ya," was all he said to his friends from Kensington, and then, never complaining, went about his life with his other horses. He and his wife owned a small farm just outside of town that they bought so they could let several of their retired horses live out their final days in comfort and serenity.

Rob had questioned Gennie extensively on her decision not to return to school and, as she expected, had offered to help her financially so she wouldn't have to work full time and could go back to earn her diploma. He couldn't help her father win any more races, but he told Gennie he would help her do anything to get out of the track. The problem was Gennie didn't want to get out. And so Rob accepted her decision without further commentary. It seems he saw a lot of himself in Gennie, which is why he had wanted to help her change her decision, but when she didn't, he understood her more than even she did.

***

Outside of Florida and California, horse racing is not glamorous in winter. "Let's get dressed up in pretty dresses and big hats and go to the track for a cold, wet, windy day of gambling, drinking, and fun!"—said no one, ever, regarding a December track meet in Ohio. Track schedules get reduced, the best horses head south to warmer climates, and the people without those options hunker down in place and make the best of it. Many track hands get second jobs at local restaurants or fast-food joints to help pay the bills over the slow winter months. And a lot of them give up. They move on from racing to something else or move further south, where it's more tolerable to work in a barn year-round. And that makes the ones who stick around even closer to each other. Those that weather the winter together stay together. As did the heroes of this story.

***

Gennie sat on her *Racing Form* on the cold concrete stairs and watched the winning horse of the last race of the day trot into a warm reception from his groom, trainer, and the owner, Kelsey Jones, the young and snobby but beautiful daughter of one of the track's executives. The horse had been a graduation gift from Daddy, in addition to a new car. The jockey, who was at Kensington between his regular gigs at far nicer tracks, high-fived the trainer and blew a kiss to Kelsey, who returned it with a flourish of her well-manicured hand.

Gennie shook her head in disgust and switched her attention to Hank and his mount as they trotted in. A somber groom and trainer met them. Gennie watched Hank's lips and hand motions as he explained that the horse got blocked, and then once he got him out of the jam, he just wouldn't fire, and so on. She got up to leave while he was still talking so he wouldn't see her there.

She walked to the track bar to look for Carl as she did every day.

As soon as Gennie pushed the door open, sending the last flash of setting sunlight into the interior of the dark bar, Carl saw her. Her grim expression clued him into how she was feeling. He caught her eyes, nodded, then continued his conversation with the other assistant trainers. She sat silently next to him as the bartender automatically gave her a glass of Coke and asked, "How ya doin'?" without making eye contact or waiting for an answer.

After a few moments, Carl turned to her. "Where's your dad?"

"He just finished; he'll probably go around looking for more work, as if anyone will give him anything."

"Did he even place today?"

Gennie pursed her lips and shrugged. "Not even close." She exhaled a long, slow breath and studied the bubbles in her glass. Quietly, she added, "Carl, I just can't take it anymore. I don't know why he doesn't just give it up. Find something else to do. I think his time has come and gone."

"Hank would rather ride till he died than try something new at this point in his life. Racing is all he knows. It must be humiliating to him."

"To him and me both, I'd say." Gennie took a slug of her drink as though it were a shot of whiskey.

Carl's friend Ruben, a young Mexican assistant starter, walked over and took Gennie's hand. "My lady, how nice to see you again," he said in his most Latin lover–type voice, laying a sloppy kiss on the top of her hand.

Gennie recoiled in disgust. "Ruben, I don't know where you get money for alcohol, but you should spend it on buying a clue instead."

"Owww!" he wailed, leaning backward, his hand thrown to his forehead in dramatic distress. "The lady has rejected me. I am alone again!"

Carl shook his head and told him to shut up. The opening door let another streak of light in. "Scumbug's here for you," Carl said, spinning Gennie's stool back toward the bar. "Don't turn around; maybe he won't see you."

Pat's jealous coworkers nicknamed him "Scumbug" soon after he started winning at Kensington, and even though his apprentice weight allowance was long expired and the bug boy asterisk had been removed from the programs, the nickname stuck.

"Pat's not a scumbug," she said, forcing the stool loose from his grip and turning around.

"Yeah, at least he's better than your pa," Carl said under his breath and returned to his discussion with Ruben about the new two-year-old colt in barn three.

Pat gave Gennie a quick hug before sitting on the stool next to her. "How'd Hank do?" he asked.

"Nothing," she shrugged. "He didn't stand a chance. How'd you do?"

"Two wins," he said sheepishly, "with Buxter Blue and Mr. Tyler's Intermingle."

"That's great! Buxter's gotta be moving up to the stakes level now, isn't he?"

"Yeah, Rob said he'll run one more here, but then we might go up to Arlington."

"Excellent," Gennie said, taking and squeezing his hands. Buxter was one of Rob's horses under another groom's care. "When would you go to Arlington?"

Pat smiled. "Why? Will you miss me?"

Gennie frowned. "I'm just asking."

He squeezed her hands back. "At the start of the spring meet, don't worry. I think it will be for just that one race. For now, I'll buy you dinner," Pat said, keeping her hands to pull her up off the stool.

"No, thanks. I better go and check on Dad," she said, pulling away and starting toward the door. She rarely took Pat up on his offers to spend money on her.

"I'll walk you then," Pat said, grabbing the door and holding it open for her.

Carl and Ruben watched the door close after them. "I still say he's a scumbug," Carl said, and they laughed and ordered more drinks.

As soon as the door shut behind them, Pat took back her right hand. "So why does Carl hate me so much?" he asked.

"Pure jealousy. You win, you're cute, and you have a girl-friend."

"I'm cute?" he asked.

Gennie threw a fake punch at him with her free hand, and he fought back with his free hand by trying to tickle her side. In this manner, they worked their way across the parking lot. She hadn't laughed so hard in several weeks: she had almost forgotten she could. She put her arm around his waist and pulled him close to stop the tickling and to feel him solidly by her side. He put his arm around her shoulders and they walked the rest of the way in silence.

Pat left her at the door to the housing complex and promised to meet her trackside in the morning as usual. As she walked into the dirty white foyer, Gennie could hear their television from down the hall. When she entered the apartment, her father smiled and turned down the volume on *Jeopardy*. He had a soft, friendly face—round, wrinkled, and capped with a tangled mess of brown and gray hairs. "Where've ya been, hon? I was starting to worry."

"With Carl and Pat, as usual."

"I'm starting to think that Pat is giving me bad luck. I may have to put my foot down on you spending any more time with him," he warned while grinning at his daughter.

"Dad, how can you even joke about luck anymore?" Gennie asked as she went to sit on the well-worn plaid chair next to him. "Don't you think it's getting serious? Maybe it's time you try something else."

"Well, listen here, Miss Genuine Harrison, I've got All That Glitters tomorrow in the eighth." He sat back and folded his arms smugly in front of his chest.

"Oh, wow, one mount that stands a chance," she said sarcastically. "You know that doesn't matter, Dad. One not-terrible horse in one race will not change over a year of losing. Even I know that."

"All That Glitters is a good mare. Mr. O'Reilly knows that my time is due again. He knows."

Gennie cringed at his obvious criticism of her. "You know as well as I do that All That Glitters was scratched by the vet from a race last month. She's a cripple! O'Reilly knows that you're probably the only rider desperate enough to ride her because she's going to drop any time now." Gennie's glare at Hank intensified, and her voice trembled.

"Well, I guess All That Glitters and I have a lot in common then. We should get along just fine." Hank returned his attention to the TV. Gennie stared at him for a moment, her mouth poised and ready to say more, but then she just stood up and went to her room, slamming the door as her goodbye.

Inside her small refuge, she stared at the bulletin board filled with images of happy times until they became blurred by tears.

Gennie covered her face with her pillow and cried for the first time in years. There was nothing on the board from the past year—nothing at all worth remembering. The losing, the denial, Mom's abandonment, this hellhole of an apartment … It was all getting to be too much.

***

After Gennie slammed her door, Hank turned the volume up on the TV, but he still could only see his daughter's frustrated face. Her face shared his piercing eyes when she scowled at him, but the rest of her was the spitting image of her mother: the slim face and delicate nose, high cheekbones and wide, green eyes … thin lips that always seemed poised to scold someone. He realized he was seeing Sylvia—her beautiful, smiling face—and he quickly turned his attention back to the next *Jeopardy* category.

Luck Be a Lady

In horse racing, there are usually nine races a day. And what makes racing unique is that even if you lose the first eight races, there is always the hope that the ninth will be your lucky race, your opportunity to make back all that money you've lost. Chances are, it won't happen, of course, but the point is that people never give up hope. That's what keeps the sport exciting and, if we're being honest here, addictive. For people who live in the sport, that same eternal flame of hope burns through their whole career. Or in other words, if you don't carry that flame, your career is over.

Gennie woke up at 4:30 a.m. Even in the darkness, she could sense she was alone; Hank had already left. He must have been too excited to sleep. Maybe today would be the day that things would begin to change. Even she permitted herself one flicker of hope.

Gennie left the housing complex and walked to the barn area, already buzzing with activity as the sun started to rise. It had rained during the night and the morning sunshine made a sparkly mist rise from the ground. It wasn't as cold as it could have been after the rain. It seemed that spring might be on its way after all. To the east, the black storm clouds moved slowly away, leaving behind a bright blue sky. She felt herself begin to relax. The barns' white walls reflected the orange sunrise making everything glow. She deeply inhaled the familiar scents of leather, hay, and horse and let out a big sigh. She felt at home and comfortable, and ready to work.

Except for a couple of "mornin's", few people spoke, as usual. The country station was playing, so Clay must have been the first one in this morning. Gennie went about her work as a ritual, heaving the hay and buckets of food. Whenever she passed a horse, she would rub its snout or give it a reassuring pat on the neck. The horses all seemed to appreciate having a woman around. Once the horses were fed, groomed, and taped up, the ones who were going to work out got tacked up, and the exercise riders finally mounted. Gennie got up on one of Rob's old quarter horses, led the racehorse and rider to the track, and let them loose for their morning workout. With the lead rope over the saddle horn, Gennie relaxed by the track rail on her sedate horse and watched the racing day begin as the sun rose higher over the backstretch.

A small group of usual trackers was already at the rail, watching the workouts while enjoying the first cigar of the day and studying their *Racing Forms*. They greeted Gennie and, trusting her insider knowledge, asked for her advice on the day's picks. "Hmm, tough one today. But I'd have to go with All That Glitters in the eighth," she said. A quick glance at their programs let them in on the joke, and they smiled and walked away, wishing her luck on her pick.

Maybe this was part of O'Reilly's logic. She knew having Hank Harrison listed as the jockey on a mount was a surefire way to have that horse crossed out by the serious handicappers. If his mare was good, O'Reilly could get a big payoff if the crowd was betting against her because of Hank's involvement. Gennie wouldn't put it past that creep of a trainer.

After the exercise rides, the horses cooled down, and the tack was taken off and carefully stored, the riders and grooms gathered in the backstretch diner for their late breakfast and daily predictions. Gennie overheard several voices saying "All That Glitters" and knew that her father was once again the topic of discussion for the underground backstretch betting pool for when Hank would finally break his losing streak.

People began filling the stands in time for the first race at one o'clock. The Saturday crowd was made up of the usual cast of characters: retired men wearing high black socks, older women adjusting their bifocals to pick their favorite horse names from the program, college kids thinking that today was the day they could win enough to afford more than ramen for dinner, and professional bettors who ignored everyone else. They all hustled to the betting windows, paddock, or food court in one big, seemingly choreographed production. An overhead shot of the scene would look like one of those old-time movies with the synchronized swimming routines. But we digress.

The noise level rose consistently with each race, peaking at the featured eighth race, when the older people began to tire, and the younger ones began thinking of their evening plans.

Pat's mount for the eighth had been scratched earlier in the day due to a hoof problem. He joined Gennie at a rail spot just as All That Glitters and Hank paraded by with the other contenders. Hank raised his crop to his daughter, who stared at him coldly. Pat took her hand and squeezed it. "At least All That Glitters isn't limping," he said hopefully. He received no response. Mr. O'Reilly took his seat in a reserved box with the owner of All That Glitters. The track's jumbotron showed odds of 16-1 for Hank's mount. Only one other entry had worse odds. Six of the other horses had better ones.

Carl prepared the staff of starters to tend to the horses as they came to the gate. Eight horses and their riders entered the starting slots one by one. The assistant starters linked arms and became human bulldozers to push reluctant horses into their "holes". All That Glitters was the only one that gave them a hard time. Once the horses were finally in the starting gate, the eight riders focused straight in front of them. The horses' nostrils flared, hooves stomped, and tails twitched. The long dirt road ahead glimmered as the sun still shone bright in the early spring sky. The bell rang, and the stillness erupted into a fury of pounding hooves, shouting jockeys, and flying colors.

All That Glitters and Hank had a clean break and stayed to the outside, in the middle of the pack. In front of them, two other mares dueled for the lead until they tired each other out, and both fell back. A third contender flew past them, seemingly laughing until it realized that there were still four furlongs to go. It sighed and gave up as quickly as it had launched. Hank held All That Glitters steady as he watched the leaders tire. Then, with a confirming switch of his stick, All That Glitters burst past the faltering leaders, showing energy only Hank knew she had in her. Hank and his flying mount crossed the finish line easily two lengths in front of his next challengers.

It was that easy. That quick. That final.

Pat dropped Gennie's damp hand. Gennie stared wide-eyed and silently as the horses began loping around the track to cool down. There was no doubt that Hank had won, no doubt that there would be no objection from any of the other riders, no doubt that the losing streak was over. A clean, easy victory. A solid win. At last. And on a long shot, to boot. But one win in nearly three hundred rides didn't mean anything, except maybe a chance at another new beginning, something the Harrisons needed badly. Gennie slowly became aware of the crowd's roar of congratulations. Although only a few of these strangers cashed in on the long-shot victory, the crowd always cheered for the underdogs who beat the odds. The other riders exchanged high fives with Hank before dismounting. The announcer even congratulated Hank over the intercom for all to hear. As All That Glitters and Hank trotted back to the winner's circle, he lifted his eyes to heaven and raised his whip in victory. Those closest to him might have seen how moist his shining gray eyes were. Even those farthest away could see his smile. At last, a woman—well, OK, a mare—had done him right. Luck was finally back riding with him.

***

When the clock hit 8:00 p.m., Gennie was out of there. She'd been waiting at the apartment for Hank to grab dinner but screw it: she was starving. She'd already passed up an invite from Pat for dinner, she assumed Hank and Carl were hanging out at the bar, and the track diner was already closed. She threw on a sweatshirt and stomped outside for the long, lonely trek to O'Casey's, a restaurant about a mile or two from the track. A lot of the backstretch employees worked in their kitchen as their second job, especially over the slow winter season. Maybe she'd get lucky and run into one to get her a friends-and-family discount.

In the morning, O'Casey's serviced the local commuting professionals who stopped for breakfast on their way to their downtown jobs. But starting in the late afternoon, the place was taken over by the students from St. Joe's, a nearby private high school. If you felt like being seen or doing the looking, you sat in the front section with the small round tables where you could watch everyone coming in through the big windows. If you were an adult who had stopped here because you didn't have time to pack a lunch or didn't have anyone to make you dinner, you went to the chrome dining counter and made friends with the owner, who often waited that section himself. If you wanted to be alone or to be alone with someone else, you went to the back dining room that had tall booths upholstered in dark red leather and hoped that at least a server would know you were there.

The whole place smelled like sizzling burgers and fried potatoes. There was a constant buzz of noise from the cooks talking and laughing loudly from the open kitchen behind the counter to the steaming cappuccino maker, to the retro-cool jukebox ironically pumping out the latest hits, to the usual din of gossip and banter coming from the patrons themselves.

Gennie took a seat at the counter, unsuccessfully scanned the kitchen crew to see if she knew anyone, ordered a burger and shake, and then changed her order to a burger with just water when she realized she had only seven dollars in her wallet.

When she finished re-reading everything she could on the menu, she put it down and tried to discreetly watch the other teens at the tables who seemed so different from her. Groups of two or four, some mixed couples, some all guys, and some all girls, exchanged jokes and gossip. Gennie was the only one in the place eating alone. The other kids all looked slick and cool in their brand-name T-shirts and jeans, as though they had just walked out of a black-and-white ad in some oversized fashion magazine. They all seemed to have perfect teeth, shiny hair, and big eyes—all the better to occasionally glance Gennie's way and then whisper to a friend.

Gennie looked down at her dirty track sweatshirt, worn, tight jeans, and nearly black tennis shoes. She felt her hair grow heavy with dullness and track grime and her skin glisten with sweat as the whispers seemed to roar in her ears.

The kids all seemed to have so much to talk about. Spring was approaching, so they must be sharing their vacation plans for spring break or discussing who's going to ask who to prom or some other equally important topic in their privileged little universe. Gennie mentally reminisced about her high school days, which were spent quietly in solitude at the public school so that she could get back quickly to the track each day. She had been a loner by choice and liked it that way.

But these kids all seemed to like each other. They laughed and waved to each other across the room. They teased the waitress, who laughed at them and knew them by name. Gennie didn't remember having fun like that in her school days. But she hadn't sought it out either. Suddenly, she started thinking that she might have made a mistake. It was only one more year, after all. Could she still get in for the second semester and finish at an accelerated pace? Then she saw two exceptionally pretty, well-dressed girls look her way, quickly turn back, and laugh.

Gennie seethed. Screw them. Why would she want to hang with a bunch of immature spoiled brats who had no idea there were problems and struggles in the world? These kids had never worked a day in their lives and thought a crisis was when they couldn't borrow Daddy's car for Saturday night. Their biggest cause was saving whales by buying cute shirts and hats as a fundraiser. When her burger came, she asked for it to go instead. She walked past the tables filled with curious eyes without looking back. She made the long walk back to Kensington at a brisk pace, with her mind racing until she got to the track grounds, across the parking lot, and then through the unlocked gate to sit on the empty benches by the rail. She unwrapped the burger, already cold, and ate in the darkened backstretch, alone in the stands but at home.

***

Gennie was preparing for bed when the apartment door opened, and Hank entered, smelling of the track bar and wearing a grin from ear to ear. "Gennie, today was the start of something special," he said. "I've got Glamour Boy and Tuscany tomorrow! Both of them can win!"

"How'd you manage that?" she asked coldly.

"Theo could tell I just had a temporary bit of bad luck. He knows I'm back on now."

"Theo? OK, what's the catch? He wouldn't let you ride his worst nag last month."

Hank smiled and shook his head. "How'd you get to be so cynical? Or intuitive. Maybe I'm not working for the full percent yet, but it's a way to get his trust back."

"Theo is a criminal. Jesus, Dad, is he giving you at least half?"

"Of course he's giving me at least half. Do you think I'm a chump? Other trainers will see me winning, and then I'll start getting the better mounts." Hank plopped himself down on the sleeper sofa and began removing his boots. Gennie could tell the discussion was over and went to her room for another restless night spent trying to sleep. She wasn't sure why she was so mad at her dad. Shouldn't she be happy for him? Maybe today was the start of something better. Why couldn't she let herself go and enjoy his excitement? Why couldn't she believe it for once?

Because, dear readers, Gennie was wise beyond her years.

**

She watched the race closely, as only experienced trackers can, clearly distinguishing the silk colors and the riders' body movements that showed their skill or desperation. Despite not having many material belongings, the Harrisons owned a high-quality pair of binoculars for race watching. Through them, she could notice one rider in the back of the pack making a slight move toward an inside hole or another rider swinging to the outside as a last attempt at a free ride home. She could always tell if the lead horse had enough strength or willpower to hold on for a win, and it was easy to see a horse that should have won but was blocked of the opportunity.

She could see her father was purposely holding onto the third-place position; his horse had more left in him for the asking. She could see the two lead riders working extra hard in the saddle, whipping and yelling and praying with all their might. They would never make it. Hank sat calmly, patiently waiting for the end of the mile to come to him. Gennie watched as her father smoothly passed the two horses in the stretch and brought his horse in a length ahead of the rest, with plenty of energy left in both of them.

Gennie watched from a distance as the riders brought their horses back to the stands, the bettors dispensed of losing tickets, and the big numbers were shown on the tote board. Hank was in the winner's circle again, this time shaking Theo's hand, then Pat's, as he passed by on his losing mount. Hank nodded at Pat and quickly glanced up as if looking for Gennie. She ducked instinctively and let herself be absorbed by the crowd. It didn't really count as another win—only a partial win since Theo was docking part of the standard winning rider bonus. But it counted for something: she just wasn't sure what yet.

Later in the afternoon, after she witnessed Hank's third win in a row, Gennie saw him by the barns as he was making more deals with trainers. She could understand the transactions from a distance thanks to her father's ear-to-ear grin and the trainers' approving nods and slaps on the back. And the handshakes, the tipping of the hats, the thumbs-up. The trainers could always smell who was full of luck in any given week and would flock to whomever it was as quickly as possible. Despite their best intentions, Gennie knew they were setting Hank up higher and higher to fall even harder as soon as this streak ended. That's the one guaranteed thing about luck: it never sticks around.

Hank caught a glimpse of Gennie in the barn and came darting over. "Gennie, let's go out and celebrate!" he exclaimed, holding up a wad of bills. "Dinner at Antoine's tonight!"

She smiled at his boyish enthusiasm but then quickly scowled at him. "We could buy a week's worth of groceries instead. Let's go shopping and save some of the money."

"Don't worry so much, little girl!" he scowled back. "I've already got two rides tomorrow, and I haven't even called Theo yet. I'll probably have at least four tomorrow, including Gogetem! We'll be eatin' out every night! Let's get Carl and—" Her stare silenced him. "Dang, you're a downer. Fine, we'll make dinner."

At home, the father and daughter worked jointly, yet silently, to make a spaghetti feast. Hank stewed the sauce with fresh green peppers, tomatoes, and as many spices as he could find, and Gennie tossed a colorful salad in the biggest bowl they owned. Carl showed up with a bottle of red wine and a loaf of Italian bread. They spent the night talking about the day's races and other track gossip, including who was the new victim of a bad luck curse. Gennie snuck out as the two tipsy veterans got more elaborate and boisterous in their tales of woe and victory.

Pat only lived in the employee dorms because it was conveniently close to work. He could afford an apartment in the city, but why should he get up even earlier in the morning to drive to work when he could sleep twenty extra minutes and walk to the barns instead? He lived alone at the far end of the complex in a clean yet barren two-room apartment. It was only a three-minute walk from Gennie and Hank's place.

Gennie knew the walk instinctively, shutting her eyes for a few moments to prove it to herself. It was in those few minutes that someone stepped in front of her. She cried out in embarrassment as she opened her eyes and nearly collided with the body in front of her. Pat was standing face to face with her and grabbed her elbows to stabilize her.

"God, you scared me to death!" she scolded angrily.

"You shouldn't be walking around with your eyes closed, then," he said, taking advantage of his stance to kiss her. It caught her off guard, but after catching her breath, she relaxed into his arms. She looked around to see if anyone saw them, only to be greeted by an empty parking lot.

"You'll get me in trouble pulling stunts like that," she said, turning to walk toward his apartment.

"That's the kind of guy I am," he said, catching up to her and putting his arm around her shoulder. "You going somewhere?"

"Well, I was hoping to find a gentleman for some evening conversation and perhaps a cup of coffee, but I suppose you will do instead."

"Good thing I bumped into you, then," he said while opening his door. A stained and dented teapot was sitting on his hot plate. He filled it with water and heated it while looking for his jar of instant coffee. "What's Hank doing tonight?"

"We made dinner, and now he and Carl are drinking and yacking away. He'll have to sit in the sweat box an hour tomorrow morning."

"How is he … mentally?"

"Well, of course, he thinks he's the greatest rider since Shoemaker again. He thinks it's all due to natural talent and skill and God's gift that he's winning. He has no idea that it's just luck and good mounts getting him by."

Pat laughed. "You're so hard on that guy. Don't you have any faith in him? Don't you think he has any talent? Does it all have to be just luck?"

Gennie put her head down and thought for a few moments. "You're right. He has talent, and it does take more than luck to win a race, but I know for a fact he was a much better rider years ago. As he gets older, he gets a little less … good. He won't admit to the physical demands of this game, so he can't see why he shouldn't be as good now as he was when he was nineteen."

"You're right; I can see that. He should probably consider retiring from riding and getting into training, the track office, or something."

"Wrong. By doing that, he would be admitting that he's not a young, skilled, desirable rider anymore. He would be admitting that he's an aging, desperate tracker. And, seriously, can you see him working in an office all day? No way."

Pat nodded. "You're probably right," he said, "but I don't think he's done yet." He stirred their coffees and brought one to her. They talked for an hour more about her father, the track, and his card for the next day. At ten, she left with a simple good-bye kiss and a long hug. She would see him again at five the next morning in the stables.

The Lady Is a Tramp

Twenty years ago, Hank Harrison came to Thistledown Rack Track look-
ing for work, and trainer Rob Wayne took him in. After a year of walking
hots, he graduated to exercise riding. When Wayne saw Harrison's way
with his horses, he encouraged him to take on race riding. After six months
of being the top rider at Thistledown, Harrison left to become the hottest
bug boy on the East Coast. He topped the rider standings at Belmont Park
for an entire season. His mounts won over a million dollars the first year
after his apprenticeship. He won the Whitney, the Gulf Stakes, and the
Blue Grass Stakes. At age twenty-five, Harrison decided to cut back his
traveling schedule to spend more time with his new family. He settled into a
comfortable and slower-paced life back at Kensington Downs, where he dom-
inated the standings for several years. But as he entered his thirties, his
winning percentage started to drop. He slipped in the standings and then
skidded into a losing streak that lasted for over two years. And now, at age
forty-two, Harrison has made a comeback befitting the champion he once
was. He's won forty of his last sixty starts at Kensington, including the
Kensington Classic on Crimson Dance. His purses have totaled more this
past month than his previous five years combined. Harrison is back and
looking to stay hot for this weekend's Chantilly Stakes when he will be
back with Rob Wayne to ride his promising colt Shawdaddy.

Gennie admired the winner's circle shot of her father upon
Crimson Dance, then put the local newspaper down to reach

for her scissors. That Kensington Classic brought them a share of a winning purse that could buy a nice car. It was nice to have a new clipping for her bulletin board finally.

Rob had made his first mount offer to Hank in three years for the Chantilly Stakes. Shawdaddy was only the track handicapper's third choice to win, but with a bit of skill, patience, and luck, the right rider could bring him in on top. Gennie smiled at the thought of Rob and Hank working together again. Maybe things were turning around.

The day of the Chantilly was the first hot and humid day of the year. The bright sun seemed to be enjoying coming out of its spring shell and showing off what it was capable of once again. Some female track visitors took advantage of the return to summer to don sun dresses with fancy hats—not Louisville Downs fancy, of course, but fancy by Kensington standards.

Gennie waited at the rail, holding one hand over her eyes, protecting them from the sunshine so she could read the program and study the field. Pat was also riding in the race on the popular favorite shipped in from Illinois just for this race. Carl was at the starting gate. Hank and Rob were yucking it up in the paddock like old times, with the three dark years quickly forgiven and forgotten, as track men were prone to do.

Gennie heard someone behind her say, "She's down there, in the blue." She instinctively froze. Why did she know they were talking about her when hundreds of others surrounded her? But she did know. And she didn't want to turn around. She stayed with her head down, moving her hand lower to cover her eyes. She wasn't sure why. Was it the FBI investigating Hank? Was it the press? Was it her old high school principal finally checking up on her?

"Gennie!" a woman's voice squealed, and Gennie realized her instincts had been correct. She suddenly wanted to dissolve into the soft dirt track in front of her. She realized instantly that she should have been preparing herself for this moment but had honestly not imagined it. She mentally kicked herself for not being ready for this because, of course—it was apparent—her mother had returned now that Hank was winning again.

"How are you?" the towering, smiling, made-up blonde asked loudly enough for the others along the rail to hear as she took Gennie in her arms for a quick, unreturned hug. "How silly—you're fine, obviously!"

Gennie stayed stiff with her mouth still hanging open, looking at Sylvia, who appeared in all her splendor with even blonder-than-usual hair, redder-than-tomatoes lipstick, and jeans designed for teenagers, not thirty-somethings. Sylvia reached out her arms, expecting Gennie to take her hands, but Gennie tightened her lips and turned back to her program. "Hello, Sylvia," she said dryly, intently watching the post-parade and hoping that her father would be too busy bragging to the ponyboy to look for her in the crowd.

"Oh, you look so healthy! How's school? Did you do well last year? You're on summer break now, of course. Oh my gosh, are you starting college next year?"

"I didn't go last year. Too busy working. Kinda weird you didn't know that, huh?"

Sylvia paused temporarily, raised her well-shaped eyebrows, and dove back in. "Oh! There's Hank! I hear he's doing so well now. I can't wait to say hi."

Hank trotted by on his horse, not bragging as Gennie had expected but actually deep in thought. He looked serious, plotting his strategy for the mile ahead.

"Oh, and there's Pat," Sylvia said with a smile. "I always thought you two would make a beautiful couple. Is he still doing well, too?"

"Very well, thank you," Gennie answered. Pat, who always looked for Gennie along the rail, smiled at her and then saw Sylvia. Even with the shade under his cap, Gennie could see his eyes widen and his chin drop. He was caught off guard when his lead pony started to trot. He quickly regained his balance and tried to get his concentration back. The bettors around her chuckled about a jocks' chances of winning when he could barely stay balanced during the post-parade.

Sylvia continued to chat incessantly even after the race had begun, but not once did she mention her absence or try to make an excuse for not calling or writing—except for a birthday card—or caring. Gennie barely heard a thing other than the pounding hooves of the approaching herd. "My, that horse won easily!" Sylvia squealed. "Oh, that was Hank! How wonderful! You must be so proud."

Hank had won the Chantilly by four lengths. Pat had finished sixth; only Gennie knew it was Sylvia's fault. She knew that seeing Sylvia broke Pat's concentration for the race. She wondered what lie Pat would make up to tell the horse's trainer.

"Well, honey, we really need to get caught up. I know you must be awful busy, but I sure would like to have you over for dinner tonight. I just got back to town, and if steak is still your favorite, please say yes, honey. I know I have a lot of explaining to do, and I'd really like it if you gave me a chance."

Gennie stared at her dumbfounded, shocked, and speechless. If steak is still your favorite, please say yes, honey? Not, let me try to explain how a mother abandons her only child for a year? Or, please come over so I can beg forgiveness and try, just try, to explain what was in my stupid little head? In Gennie's peripheral vision, she could see the winning entourage approaching the winner's circle for the traditional photograph. She quickly nodded her head, hoping that would get Sylvia to leave.

"OK, awesome!" Sylvia smiled.

Gennie thought, My, what big teeth you have.

"I'll pick you up here at six, OK? By the main entrance? I can't wait." Sylvia left without giving Gennie a chance to object, but Gennie didn't mind as soon as she saw Sylvia exiting the grounds without approaching the winner's circle to see Hank. She watched the woman who abandoned her weave gracefully through the crowd until she disappeared.

She thought this would hurt her father even more than losing again. Would Hank feel that Sylvia's return proved that he was worthy again of being victorious in all areas of happiness? He never spoke about Sylvia once she had left, so Gennie wasn't sure if he blamed himself and his losing ways for her departure or if he saw Sylvia as the reason he became a loser in the first place. Maybe her absence had been the lucky charm he needed. Gennie turned toward the winner's circle just as Hank raised his whip in a victory greeting to her. She smiled weakly back at him and then at Pat, who shook his head as he walked behind her father. She was sure it was about Sylvia's return and not his disappointing finish in the stakes race.

All or Nothing at All

Some readers might think there's no way a mother would walk out on her teenage daughter and disappear for over a year, but in this case, it happened. Sylvia, of course, is not unique among women. It's happened through the ages, and many a child has persevered to overcome it and go on to great things, and then write books or screenplays about it. Although it's perhaps more common for men to have mid-life crises, it can happen to women, especially women like Sylvia, who'd had such a dramatic change in circumstances over her three-plus decades. Oh, the historical novels always make giving up worldly possessions for love sound so honorable and romantic. Still, those authors rarely flash forward to twenty years later to see how that former princess is enjoying that tiny unheated apartment and four crying children now while the romantic male lead is toiling away at a meaningless job that keeps him away from home for long hours, so he doesn't have to see the disappointment in his wife's eyes any more than necessary.

Sylvia just "broke", is all. She couldn't take it. She didn't have the mental strength or energy to shoulder the reality of her situation changing over time. You don't hear much about women like her because, well, who wants to? We want to hear about the heroes, survivors, and overachievers who do extraordinary things when not expected to. We don't want to hear about those who fail in their duties; who don't live up to expectations; who don't succeed at even the most basic task of parenting a child; those who change their minds mid-life and flee; those who don't take oaths and promises as seriously as do most other decent human beings.

But even those women sometimes wake up from their new daydreams and realize what they left behind. Maybe it's too late for their survivors to take them back. Or sometimes, maybe it's not. It just depends on the individual situation.

And, if we're being real here, some of these women realize that it's more complicated than expected to start over after they take these significant mid-life risks. They can't afford it. They get abandoned by their new Prince Charming. The new trail they hoped to blaze was just another dead end.

***

Gennie glanced over her shoulder to make sure no one else was around in the empty parking lot after the races were long over. A few folks were still leaving the diner, but they were far enough away that she couldn't see their faces, nor could they see hers. Sylvia pulled up in a black SUV; it was a few years old but still in good shape. She wore a tight tank top, revealing that she must be working out again. Her hair was up in a messy ponytail bun. Gennie wasn't sure if she had done it in a hurry or if she was trying to look like a teenager. Gennie noticed the layers of makeup that Sylvia had applied, obviously trying to hide the lines and crevices that were beginning to show on her face.

Gennie slid into the black leather seat, and the automatic seat belt immediately began to tie her down. "So, Gennie," Sylvia said, shaking her head and smiling. "We certainly have a lot of catching up to do, but first, I have to apologize for not keeping in touch." She started driving toward downtown.

Gennie's mind flashed back to her freshman yearbook and how all the girls had signed it. "Keep in touch, OK?" She was surprised to hear herself say, "Yeah, Sylvia, most mothers do usually keep in touch."

"Well, now, before you go and judge me without knowing really a thing about me, you need to know that I am a woman who's accustomed to a certain way of living, and Hank … well, Hank didn't seem to understand that. He just never even tried. He made me promises that he never kept, really. So, basically, Gennie, he didn't even try to help me, so in a way, it was him who deserted me when I really, really needed him." She kept her eyes on the road, so she didn't have to meet Gennie's glare.

"Are you still with Bruce?" Gennie asked coldly.

"Well," Sylvia said, forcing a bigger smile and shaking her head while keeping her eyes straight ahead, "Bruce was doing really well, and I guess a lot of women like that in a man. Uh, and last time I checked, he's still seeing a college girl. Oh, here we are."

Gennie was surprised to see her stop at the prestigious Ravenswood Hotel. Gennie knew that was where the big league trainers stayed when they came to town. Her mother tossed the keys playfully to a young valet with a wink. They went through the shining chrome and black lobby and up the elevator to the tenth floor. The room turned out to be a suite, complete with a kitchen, living room, and spacious bedroom. Everything was modern and sleek, and clean. Patio doors lead out to a fantastic view of the city. A patio table was set with white roses in a silver vase.

"You still working for Grandpa?" Gennie asked, looking about the fancy room.

"Yes," Sylvia said from the kitchen, scurrying about with her dinner preparations. "I've opened a few new restaurants for him. They're doing well! I wasn't sure I'd enjoy getting back into the workforce, but it's sort of fun—especially doing it as a boss. I thought we would eat outside since it's so nice tonight, and then maybe a game of Monopoly, hmm?" she called from the kitchen nook. Gennie's eyes scanned the interior until she found the game, still shrink-wrapped, on the coffee table. Monopoly had been her favorite game when she was younger, and Sylvia had at least remembered that. Gennie didn't know what had happened to her copy of the game. It must have been left behind in the move, or Hank might have donated it to the jockey's room game shelves.

Sylvia was in the kitchen only a few minutes before she brought out mounds of food to the table. Steaks, potatoes, green beans with almonds in a cream sauce, warm muffins, and red wine. She obviously had brought everything from one of her restaurants in advance; there was no way she could have made it all. And cooking had never been her forte. But even if she had purchased it all, the restaurant business had given her a knack for coordinating a good meal, Gennie thought, admiring the spread.

"Does Hank let you drink wine?" she asked, winking. Gennie shook her head no and claimed to have sulfite allergies. She knew she needed to keep her wits about her for this visit. Sylvia poured the wine for herself and got Gennie some iced tea instead. For dessert, Sylvia made root beer floats, another of Gennie's childhood favorites, complete with paper straws.

They exchanged few words while they ate. Gennie devoured all she could—everything was delicious. "This was really great," she admitted, slurping the last of her float. "The steak was perfect." As soon as she said it, she realized she had set her first foot into Sylvia's trap.

Sylvia smiled with her lips pursed and her eyes beaming. "Oh, thanks, honey. I'm so glad you liked it. Monopoly now?"

"I can't stay that long," she replied as she scanned the room again. "Are you moving back here?" she asked.

"Oh, no, I'll just be here a few months, maybe. I'm opening a restaurant for Daddy here. Then I'll probably go back to St. Louis. Daddy's opening up a new restaurant there next year." She winked at Gennie and picked up their dirty dishes.

"How is Grandpa?"

"Oh, you know, he's still a tough little cookie, even at his age. But he's at least talking to me again and helping me out."

"Since you left Hank, right?"

"Well … it's true he never loved Hank, but with Mamma's death and all, I think it was just such a big shock to him, and he wanted me to stay with him, you know? 'Daddy's little girl' and all that. He just wanted our life to stay the way it was."

Gennie knew she was lying. She had heard from Carl that Sylvia's father hated Hank as soon as he laid eyes on him and blamed Hank for keeping Sylvia from going to college. Grandpa Trudeau had never once even acknowledged Gennie's existence. She had heard of him only as a folktale. She realized for the first time over that dinner that her mother got many of her traits from her bloodlines.

"So, you're just passing through, then?" Gennie asked.

"Yeah, in a sense. Well, of course, I wanted to check in on you and Hank and see how things are going for you. My first day here, I saw Hank's photo in the newspaper and was so happy for him. But I don't know that he'll even want to see me.

73

He's such a proud man; he probably won't …" Her voice faded as she looked up to Gennie to answer her fears.

"Well, uh, right now might be a bad time. You're right. I'll let you know, maybe in a few days, if I think it's a good time. Oh, but speaking of Hank, I've got to get back home. He'll be panicked." Gennie hurried to her feet and the door.

"But we didn't even …" Sylvia started.

"There are a lot of things we haven't done," Gennie said more harshly than she realized she had the strength to say. "It's almost nine; the buses run on the hour." Gennie headed to the door.

"Don't be silly, I'll drive you back home. And I will take you up on the offer to play some other time. I want to see you as much as possible as long as I'm here," Sylvia announced.

"No," she snapped. She saw her mother's face fall for the first time that night. She looked truly sad. Gennie started again, "I mean, OK, we'll get together, but really, I'll take the bus home tonight. It's not far, and I have tokens. Gotta go." Gennie darted down the hall, proud of herself for avoiding Sylvia's hugs again, leaving her mother standing hopelessly at the door, holding her car keys in one hand and looking disappointed.

Gennie barely remembered getting on the bus. She must have been waiting a while. Must have put the tokens in the slot. Must have chosen a seat on the mostly empty bus. Must have looked out the window to watch the locations pass so she would know when to rise to signal, "This is where I get off." But Gennie's mind was too busy racing with memories and questions. What if Sylvia had never left? What if Sylvia had gone back to work sooner to help their family during the lean times? Would Gennie have stopped working at the track and become a "normal" teenager, working at her grandfather's restaurants instead, getting good grades, hanging out at O'Casey's with girls and guys her age, and checking out and judging strangers as they entered? What if her long-lost grandfather decided to take Gennie under his wing and make her a manager like Sylvia? What if Hank saw Sylvia and killed her? What if Hank saw Sylvia and reunited with her? Would Sylvia still like Pat? Would Sylvia hit on Pat? What would Hank do if he found out where Gennie had been that night? Would Carl approve of her visit? Would he tell Hank if Gennie confided in him? Was the word "sorry" in her mother's vocabulary? Why hadn't she once apologized or even acknowledged abandoning her daughter? All she had talked about was leaving Hank. What about leaving your only child? How much forgiveness is a child required to have?

Gennie realized that Sylvia was the reason she would never have children. She might never even have sex to avoid the risk of ever even accidentally having children. Sorry, Pat. If bad mother genes like that existed in the world, they ran in her family, and she would never wish that upon another kid. Maybe she should admit right now that she would never settle down. Never take a chance on a husband, and definitely not a family. Should she end things with Pat right now to avoid disappointing him?

Oh my God, was that root beer spiked? Gennie finally became aware of her racing pulse and heart. She took a few long, deep breaths to try and calm down.

Gennie watched the busy city streets roll past the window and slowly transform into deserted and darkened roads. By the time her stop came, she was the only one left on the bus. The driver wished her a good night, and she walked back to the track through the deserted parking lot with only all the voices in her head to keep her company.

Little White Lies

Sunday morning. Although many people viewed it as the day of rest or religious contemplation, in horse racing, Sunday is just another day at the races—except maybe for a Catholic mass being on the radio in the barn in the morning. On this particular Sunday, Gennie woke up before the alarm went off and stared into the darkness for a while before sighing, getting out of bed, and starting the day. She was able to get dressed and ready quickly, mostly in the dark, but as she tried to exit the apartment quietly, Hank called out from the couch, "Kind of surprised to see you up so early when you got in so late."

Gennie flinched and nearly dropped her keys. She turned to look at him with an exaggerated, fake smile that he most likely couldn't even see in the dark. "Oh, good morning. Yeah, Pat and I went to that new restaurant in town. We had to wait a long time for a table—really crowded. OK, see you in a bit. Have a good day." She shut the door quickly but rested against it to take a few breaths before walking away. She never lied to Hank. She might not tell him everything, but she had never had to lie before. She didn't like it but didn't know what else to do. She shook it off and went to work.

Being with the horses gave her more time to think and sort things out in her head. Each of her horses got extra long grooming sessions as she used the time to imagine different scenarios of what might happen while Sylvia was in town. With each brush stroke on a horse's back, she could picture a potential disaster. With every hoof pick, Gennie remembered something that Sylvia had done to make her mad. With every comb stroke on a mane or tail, she thought of her father's delicate mental constitution. The horses seemed to like the extra attention and sometimes would turn their heads to look at Gennie as though they wanted to ask her what was up, but then they would return to their relaxed state of simply enjoying the pampering.

She saw Pat in the tack room and instead of the usual good morning greeting, she grabbed his wrist and whispered, "Can you meet me for breakfast at ten?"

He looked startled and confused but quickly said, "Yeah, sure, of course," and Gennie darted away before he could ask any questions.

Pat was waiting for her at ten as directed. When she arrived, she motioned for him to move to the table at the far back of the room. As she walked through the diner, she smiled and said hi to other trackers while scanning the room to make sure Hank or his closest cronies weren't there. Once seated, she poured out the events of the past evening. Pat listened with a furrowed brow and his fingers tapping back and forth on the table. They were so engrossed in the story that neither one saw Carl enter and sit at the counter, watching them both and their seemingly intent discussion from his stool. Once the waitress poured him his first cup of coffee, he called Gennie's name. She jumped and spun around in her seat to see Carl motioning for her to come over. There was an empty stool next to him.

She turned back to Pat and shrugged. "Well, I lied to Hank, but I can't lie to Carl. I'll just get it over with." Pat nodded and watched her walk over. His eyes met Carl's as he was also watching Gennie, and Carl glared at Pat until he got uncomfortable and threw up his hands in surrender. Carl just looked away toward Gennie as she sat next to him like a scolded schoolgirl.

"Hey, your pa said you were at Pat's place 'til all hours last night," he said accusingly. "You're only seventeen, and you gotta remember that he's older, and no matter what a 'nice guy' you think he is—"

"I wasn't with Pat last night," she said, facing the counter to avoid his eyes.

"What are you talking about? Where were you?"

"At your aunt's fancy hotel suite for dinner."

He scrunched his face, trying to understand. "Huh?"

"Sylvia's back."

He reeled back as if he'd been hit. "Oh, holy Christ, I shoulda known she'd come crawling back. Like we need any more drama in this family." He slammed his coffee and motioned to the waitress for another refill. "So, what's she up to? Is she living here or just visiting?"

"Just visiting for a while, I guess. She wined and dined me and asked if I thought Hank would want to see her, and I told her now wouldn't be a good time."

"Good, good thinking. Man, she could blow all of Hank's concentration and end his career right here, right now. We gotta keep her away."

"Yeah, I know," Gennie said, standing up. "I'll handle it. I've got to go finish some things up for Rob." As she walked to the exit, Pat got up and accompanied her. Carl watched them leave and then followed behind, leaving a few dollars and half a cup of coffee on the counter.

That day Hank brought in three winners out of five mounts. He grinned proudly at Gennie and gave her the $200 she needed to buy the new pair of boots she had been wanting. At first, she resisted, saying they should be saving some money for the future, but then she realized she hadn't bought anything new in over a year, her current boots' heels were worn down, and the soles were getting dangerously thin. She had Carl drive her to the saddlery store on the outskirts of town to buy the shiny black boots with cash. When they got home, she polished them with saddle soap for an hour until the leather began to loosen.

Hank beamed as he entered the apartment and saw her hard at work on the boots. She looked up and couldn't help but smile. "Thank you," she said. "They're wonderful."

"Maybe you can wear them when you lead me for the Kensington Mile," he said with a wink.

"You got a mount for the Mile?" she asked, sticking her fingers into the soap instead of using the rag. With all of Hank's recent luck, he had yet to win a graded stakes race. The Mile was the one Kensington Race a year that got covered by network TV. In their little world, it was a pretty big deal.

"All That Glitters is ready for it," he said, "and Mr. O'Reilly knows I'm the only one she'll run for."

"All That Glitters again? Are you sure she's fit? That last race seemed to take a lot out of her."

"Oh, she'll be the fittest of them all. I feel good about this one."

Gennie, speechless, stared at him. She had been wrong about All That Glitters last time, so maybe she should trust Hank on this one. After all, he was the one who had ridden the race, and surely he would have been able to tell if anything was wrong with that mare. She returned to scrubbing her boots as Hank sat on the couch and turned on the TV.

***

Sylvia showed up at the track on a day that Hank lost his first three races in a row, then recovered with victories in the last two. After the last race, she found Gennie with Carl at the rail and gave each of them a big hug. Sylvia suggested that they find Hank and all go out to dinner together, but Carl quickly said that Hank had a meeting with Mr. O'Reilly that night to discuss the Kensington Mile on Saturday. Sylvia's eyes lit up with the mention of the Mile, and she reminisced about Hank's first win in the stakes over fifteen years earlier. "I know what," she said. "Let's plan a victory dinner for Saturday night! Maybe you all could warm Hank up to the idea before then, and I'll meet you right here after the race. How does that sound? Oh, I can't wait to catch up with you all. OK, then? I'll see you Saturday." Sylvia practically danced up the stairs—or at least as much as her too-tight jeans would allow—and disappeared again into the crowd. Carl and Gennie just looked at each other and shook their heads.

***

The usual crowd gathered at the track bar Friday night to make each other more nervous about the big stakes day ahead. Hank got some good-natured teasing about three more losses that day. "I would have had that second race if it wasn't for Pat bumping his way through," Hank said, grinning at Gennie and Pat, who sat at the end of the largest table in the room. The track handicapper Ace Tyler reviewed the preliminary program for Saturday and crunched his forehead in concern. "Hank, I thought I heard the vet tell O'Reilly that All That Glitters shouldn't run for at least two months after that last one."

"Nah. O'Reilly is watching her real careful. She's fine; the vet'll agree."

Tyler shrugged and continued reading. Gennie looked sternly at her father, who quickly started talking about Rob's hot new colt that he had worked that morning. Carl tried to find a time all night to bring up the subject of Sylvia with Hank, but it never happened. Everyone cleared out at the same time. As she rose to leave, Gennie whispered to Carl that she would try to break the news to Hank the following morning. "No, forget it," Carl said. "Let's not jinx him for the Mile. We'll just act as surprised as he does when she shows up tomorrow night." Gennie sighed. What's another little lie, she thought, then agreed with Carl and followed the crowd back to the backstretch complex.

Cashing In

Race Day. Big Race Day. Kensington Mile Day. We can imagine the scene as one of those old black-and-white wartime news-reels, showing a wide shot of Kensington buzzing with activity. Fans in herky-jerky motion stream through the turnstiles with smiles on their faces and visions of cashing in winning tickets in their heads. Track handicappers study their *Daily Racing Form* in the early morning to set the day's odds. Close-ups of horses' nostrils flaring, hooves stomping at the ground in anticipation. The jockeys' room was filled with the small but mighty riders who would guide the day's stars to fame or failure. The trainers and owners who couldn't sleep last night were powering up on caffeine and conversation in the track diner with the only others who understood what they were going through. The whole little movie would be narrated by an overdramatic announcer: Kensington Mile Day at Kensington Downs! The one day a year when the eyes of the horse racing world focus on this little corner of Ohio …

The black-and-white film flashes and sputters as it runs out of the projector, and we return to the living color of reality, which, for once, might match the drama of a film production. The track is dry and fast, and well groomed. The backstretch is crowded, with visiting horses and their entourages shipped in especially for the Mile. Local sportscasters wander the backstretch with their cameramen to capture scenes of the preparations for the morning news shows. Grooms work extra hard on the race's star runners, brushing their coats till they shine and braiding their manes. The jockey valets polish boots for a few extra minutes. Owners and trainers wear button-down shirts instead of the standard T-shirts. The track maintenance crew waters flowers and mows the vast lawn first thing in the morning. The local Dixieland band warms up to entertain the fans in the grandstand area.

For the regulars of Kensington Downs, this was their big day, the one day of the year they were guaranteed to get a mention in the *Daily Racing Form* and on *ESPN*. Everyone and everything had to look good. The July humidity relaxed its grip so that horses and humans alike breathed easier and walked a little quicker.

The local news crews had beautiful backdrops for all their shots: Blue skies. Colorful flowers spelling out "Kensington" on the lush garden at the track's entrance. Beautiful women in sundresses and big hats. Lovely horses with their shiny groomed coats gleaming in the summer sun.

Our starlet Gennie enters the scene walking through the barns that morning to see All That Glitters. Gennie could hear her before seeing her: All That Glitters was snorting, whinnying, and stomping. Her groom carefully walked the freshly brushed bay mare and watched her every move. Gennie zeroed in on the mare's legs. She seemed fine, or, wait—was she favoring her left hind leg? Gennie watched for a few minutes and decided she looked fine. All That Glitters saw Gennie and threw her head up and down while walking and blew air loudly through her nostrils. The groom spoke gently, trying to calm her, but the horse seemed aware of all the fuss and was anxious. Only the mare knew if she was scared or nervous or excited, or hurting. Gennie watched her walk by and whispered, "Give my daddy a good ride, baby." All she got was a snort in reply.

Hank had entered the jocks' room with the pride of a peacock, wishing all his coworkers top of the morning, and then started the race day with two losses in a row. Gennie saw him hanging his freshly barbered head a little low as he walked toward the jockey room after the second race. She was concerned that the other riders would hassle him and get him more riled up for the eighth race. She had heard that once, during his losing streak, he had taken a swing at some hotshot bug boy who said something rude to him. Pat had held Hank back to avoid a full-out brawl. That was the only sign Gennie had received that losing was bringing her father down: the only sign that he wasn't an automaton. Maybe her father did have feelings he kept buried inside of him. She hoped Pat was back there to keep an eye on things.

Before the eighth race, Gennie had to maneuver through the crowd to find a spot at the paddock fence. She surveyed the other horses as they were tacked up, and the riders got their final instructions from the trainers. All That Glitters, now with all four legs bandaged, didn't want the saddle on her, and she threw herself from one side of her stall to the other. The groom and Theo had to hold her still long enough to get everything on and tightened properly. The vet spent a lot of time with her and then went up to Theo for a while to exchange words. The trainer shook his head, laughed, and patted the vet on the shoulder. They shook hands, and the vet moved on to inspect the next entry.

The riders for the featured race all came out of the jocks' room together and commented to each other about the size of the crowd and smiled for pictures that kids along the rail requested. Pat smiled for a photo while his eyes scanned the crowd for Gennie. He finally found her, her eyes focused on the horses as he expected.

Hank saw Gennie and walked over to her before heading to the paddock stall. "Here to give me some good luck, hon?" he asked.

"By the looks of it, I might be here to say our last goodbye," she said as All That Glitters reared up as the groom was trying to lead her out to Theo.

"Aw, she's just wound up for the race. She's saving some of that energy for me! Did you put any money on us?"

"Dad, you know I don't bet."

"But of all days, Gennie, I think today's something special." He reached into his back pocket and handed her a betting ticket. It was a $50 bet to win on All That Glitters. "Here, then, you hold this for me. You've always been my lucky charm. I'll see you in the winner's circle, hon." Hank winked at her, then smiled and waved to the fans surrounding her as he walked toward his horse.

"Be careful," she whispered, even though she knew he couldn't hear her. The paddock judge made the call for "Riders up!" Hank rubbed his mount's snout and told her that she was the most beautiful mare in the whole wide world, then Theo gave him a leg up onto the mare's back. He tipped his whip to Gennie as he walked by. She feebly waved the ticket at him and then put it into her back pocket. Pat rode by on his mount and smiled. She smiled at him before walking alone to the rail and squeezing through the crowd to get a spot close to the finish line. She checked the odds board and All That Glitters was still the favorite to win despite being the only female in the field. Pat's mount was the bettors' second choice. Gennie, for once, hoped that Pat didn't win. The dinner conversation tonight would be terrible if Pat was the one who burst Hank's bubble.

All That Glitters, as usual, gave Carl a hard time at the starting gate. It took three men to shove her into her stall. Once in, she tried to rear up but came down against the metal stall, nearly crushing Hank's leg. As soon as she landed, Carl opened the gates quickly before she had time to act up again.

All That Glitters swerved violently to her right as the gate opened, nearly crashing into the Number Four horse, and then rampaged her way to the front of the field. She thundered to a three-length lead and then to five lengths within the first half mile. She lowered her head to look back to see if other horses were approaching. Hank tried talking to her, attempting to hold her back to save some energy for the finish, but her ears stayed forward. She was ignoring him and concentrating only on finishing far ahead of her competitors. Or maybe she just wanted to get this over quickly so she could get back to the barn and a good pail of feed. Or perhaps she was feeling pain and thought the quicker she got to that stupid wire, the faster she could feel better. We'll never know.

After they rounded the last turn and headed down the backstretch, it became clear to Gennie that Hank didn't have control of the horse. She wasn't leading because Hank was urging her; she was leading because she was running away with him. All That Glitters, even with her comfortable lead, veered to her right and then to her left as Hank helplessly tried to tighten the reins. Just as All That Glitters thundered past Gennie, she saw that the hind left bandage was soaked with blood. With the win imminent, Gennie knew Hank was trying desperately to control the mare so he could save her life. He knew. He was using every bit of his energy to pull up on her, and just after they crossed the finish line, she reared up in a fury and that hind leg gave out.

Hank flew off the tall, flailing mare and back across the finish line he had just crossed, crashing down on his neck, then his back. All That Glitters toppled backward over him, her torso eclipsing, then crushing, the small body that had just tried to save her. The other six horses in the field panicked. Several had no choice but to swerve or dive over the immediate crash scene. One tried to slide to a stop. The horse closest behind it had no chance to stop; it fell right into All That Glitters, dumping its rider next to Hank. Pat's mount veered to its left and slammed into the rail, but Pat was able to stay aboard and in control. The track was an explosion of dust and bodies and wailing horses.

Gennie felt herself screaming, yet she didn't hear anything. She was seeing things right in front of her but couldn't move her limbs or make a noise. It was like she was watching herself from above, but she couldn't do anything about it. She could barely see through her tears to the destruction just a few yards away. She had seen spills and falls and bad accidents many times. She thought she had seen the worst of them. But what she witnessed now was beyond imagination. The crowd all pushed against her to get a better look. Spectators screamed or gasped, and a few swore under their breath. Parents rushed their children away from the scene so they wouldn't have to witness the carnage. Some trackers just went back to the betting windows for the next race, unfazed, as they knew the risk was part of the game. Some in the crowd, shocked and scarred by what they'd just seen, walked away, never to return to the track again.

A siren screamed on top of the chaotic din as the track ambulance rushed to the scene, and soon medical personnel surrounded Hank and the other fallen jockey. Someone assembled a screen to prevent the crowd from witnessing any more gruesome details. Amid the chaos, unseen hands guided Gennie by her shoulders through the crowd and onto the track. She was sobbing uncontrollably, her whole body was heaving, but she knew she had to get to Hank. Carl nodded to the security guards who let them pass and then gently whispered in her ear, "Go help him, Gennie," as she wove her way through the emergency workers. She fell to her knees and crawled to get to Hank, who was already tightly surrounded by paramedics. Carl motioned to them to let Gennie through.

Hank looked peaceful, though crumpled, with his eyes shut. "Dad," she said with sudden strength, "you won the Mile, just like you said you would. Come on now, let's go cash this ticket." Then, ever so slightly, she saw him smile, but his eyes remained closed.

Put Your Dreams Away

TV sports shows are careful not to taint the image of the sport that brings in pretty good ad revenue in the spring. When tragedy strikes, they'll quickly cut to a commercial until the carnage is cleaned up. But in those lovely Hollywood movies, you'll see dramatic slow-mo footage of the horses' eyes bright with fear, their thin legs that had just been running at full speed unexpectedly and desperately trying to stop their thousand-pound bodies from the natural laws of inertia, and then the colorful little jock on the ill-fated steed's back flying through the air. In the movies, you might see the jock's arms flailing wildly like he thinks he could take flight to avoid the cold hard earth, but in reality, riders know to try to roll into a ball. They try to make themselves even smaller than they already are with hopes of rolling away and avoiding hooves or the horse's body weight. Nine out of ten times, the jockeys are successful. They roll away, stand up, shake it off, and go to get ready for the next race. The horses usually aren't that lucky. Sometimes whatever caused the accident might be a fluke or a treatable condition, but sadly, gentle readers, there are many accidents that cause grave injury that can't be cured or mended.

In this particular incident, seen by thousands of racing fans in the stands that day and several thousand more who happened to be flipping channels on a Saturday afternoon at home, no one got lucky. Our beloved Hank did not get to walk away, and All That Glitters will shine no more. Her owner will pull all his other horses from O'Reilly's barn, and the track vet will get a stern questioning session about how he could have missed the mare's issues.

And then, the next day's racing schedule will proceed as planned.

***

Both Gennie and Carl entered his apartment silently. Gennie sat down on his worn couch and looked about at his walls, surprisingly well-covered with posters of significant horse races over the years. Gennie realized she'd never really looked at them before. Carl went to make some coffee. Thank God for coffee to give you something to do when you don't know what else to do, right? He finally came back and sat on the couch with her. She remained silent, admiring the souvenir poster from the 1982 Derby. After a few moments, Carl said, "Gennie, girl, I know this has gotta be killing you. I mean, I lost both my parents, but I was too young to really remember them."

"I didn't lose Hank. I know exactly where he is."

"Well, right, I know. Now, don't go getting all tough on me."

"I'm not. I hate that expression. I didn't 'lose' him. He hasn't 'passed on'. He's fucking dead."

By the grace of God, there was a frantic knocking at the door to break the tension—or to add to it. Pat entered before Carl even finished opening the door. Gennie slowly stood to meet him, and they hugged. She eventually pulled herself away and wiped her eyes with her sleeve. "Who was the other rider?"

"Jackie Valance. He'll be OK. Just a few broken ribs, maybe a concussion."

She nodded silently, relieved. "And All That Glitters?"

Pat shook his head. "Had to be put down."

Gennie nodded and gave a deep sigh. She sat down again, looked at both of them as they stared back at her, and quietly said, "Mom."

"I'm sure she knows about it," Carl said. "We know she was there somewhere."

"Will I have to go with her now?"

Carl and Pat looked at each other, just to avoid Gennie's lost stare.

"You're almost eighteen; you don't have do anything you don't want to. For all we know, Sylvia already left town." Carl saw Gennie sigh in honest recognition and felt bad for suggesting it, despite how true it probably was. "You're seventeen, for Chrissake," he said, standing up. "Maybe they'll give me custody."

Unintentionally, Pat let out a, "Hmph."

Carl glared at him. "Or maybe they'll let you be treated as an adult, since you're so close anyway. They do it with criminals."

Gennie stared at an old *Racing Form* that lay on the floor. She could see Hank's name in a subheading to an article. Pat sat next to her and took her hand.

"We could get married. Sylvia would just have to approve it."

Gennie flinched and stared at him in shock. "What? Get married? Now? I—"

Even Carl's mouth fell open. "Whoa, whoa, whoa. Let's not rush into any decisions yet. We'll just stay calm, and Gennie'll stay here until we hear otherwise. I'm sure Social Services will be giving me a call. I'm next of kin. Well, at least the nearest kin in town. Someone took my name at the hospital. We've had enough to think about in one day."

Pat continued staring at Gennie, holding her hand. "Seriously," he said, "we should really consider all of our options." Gennie looked at his warm brown eyes, then at the floor, at her well-oiled new boots.

Carl watched the pair for a moment, seeing the sincerity on Pat's face and the sadness on Gennie's. He left them for his bedroom, realizing they needed some time alone.

Gennie took the race ticket out of her jeans pocket and stared at it. Fifty dollars to win. What were the chances? She tore the ticket up and let it fall. Together, she and Pat watched the pieces float to the floor. Her eyes remained on the pieces as Pat just put his arm around her and guided her down to the couch where they both lay, Pat's arms surrounding her, holding her tight, and his head nestled into her hair. They didn't say another word.

Gennie tried to think of things to say. She wondered what she should be feeling now. She wondered where Sylvia was right then. Running away? Drinking in some dive bar? At the hospital looking for her? Gennie thought about rolling over and telling Pat that they should go to the courthouse tomorrow and get a wedding license. Then she imagined running away by herself and starting over somewhere totally new so her future would be up to her and not up to Pat or Sylvia or Carl or Family Services. She wondered if Hank could see her now. What would he want her to do? He definitely wouldn't want her lying on a couch, wrapped so snug and secure in Pat's arms—or maybe he actually would. He knew in his heart of hearts Pat was a good guy. She was sure of it. She wondered if her dad had felt pain in those last minutes—or was the thrill of victory strong enough to keep him feeling good? She wondered what Pat's folks would think of today's events, and of Pat's offer. Her grandfather had kicked Sylvia out of his life when at age nineteen she announced she was marrying Hank. Would Pat's family do the same to him? They seemed like good, nice people. She doubted Pat's parents would question anything he would do at this point: but she was sure they'd try to talk him out of it. Just like they had tried to get him into another profession—and look at how that worked out.

She was working up the energy to talk to Pat about all this when she felt him breathing deeply against her neck, his body heavy against her own, but his arms still tight. He was asleep, and she knew he needed his sleep. He had a full race card the next day. She hugged his hands to her chest and tried to slow her mind. She watched the room grow dark, the posters fade to unreadable, and after a few minutes she heard the coffee maker switch off automatically.

She must have eventually fallen asleep because she was startled awake by Pat's watch alarm going off near her ear at 4:30 a.m. Pat quickly hit the button off and leaned over to kiss her neck.

"How you doing?" he whispered.

She shrugged. "A little headache. I'm OK."

"Do you want me to cancel my races today? I can. No one would blame me."

Gennie knew he had some good mounts for the day. "No, you go and work. I'll have stuff I have to do today. Could you tell Rob I'm not going to be there?"

Pat smiled. "Gennie, I'm pretty sure he realizes that. Don't worry about it. Call me if you need me to help with anything, OK? I don't mind dropping the last couple of races if you need me."

"Thanks, sure, that sounds good."

He turned her toward him to look in her eyes with the early summer sunrise starting to peek through the blinds. "I love you. You know that, right?"

She studied his face, the lines, the eyes, the lips she knew so well. She nodded.

"Just take your time. Think about everything. But know that I'll do anything for you. I'd do anything to take away your pain."

She smiled despite tears welling up in her eyes and kissed him lightly. "I know," she said.

"You stay here and sleep in," he said. "You need it." He tried to get up off the lumpy couch without disturbing her and ended up accidentally jabbing her with a knee. She laughed, despite everything. Pat smiled down at her, glad to see she was still capable of a smile, and then left the apartment as quietly as he could.

Gennie rolled over into the warm spot Pat had left on the couch and grabbed the old afghan blanket that Carl had resting on the end. She covered herself and found sleep easier this time.

Take a Chance

Gennie woke with a start. She sat straight up and looked around. When she saw the room was filled with sunlight, she was confused. Where was she? What time was it? She hadn't woken up to sunlight in years. The second thing that confused her was the pounding. Lots of pounding. As her eyes adjusted to the brightness, she saw Carl, dressed, with a coffee cup in hand, going to answer the door.

Then Gennie remembered everything and lay back down. How weird, she thought. For a moment, she had forgotten everything.

Sylvia rushed into the room as soon as Carl opened the door. Her eyes were nearly as red as Gennie's, and her face looked gaunt, scared. Her hair was down, she had no makeup on, and she wore a plain pair of jeans and a restaurant T-shirt. Gennie could finally see a family resemblance and realized she must look equally crappy. Sylvia came to the couch and hugged Gennie tightly, then nodded sympathetically to Carl, who sat at his small kitchen table.

"Gennie, how ya doing, honey?" she asked, pulling away to look at her but still holding onto her hands.

"I'm OK. We've got to go and plan the funeral today. The guy at the hospital yesterday gave us a number we have to call …"

"Oh, Gennie, I'm so sorry you have to do this alone."

"She's not alone," Carl said, standing back up.

"Thank you, Carl. I really do appreciate all you've done for her. But I mean, without me, without a mother. She's too young to be handling these things." Tears streamed down her face. She let out a long breath. Gennie wasn't sure if it was a sigh or if she couldn't breathe. "Gennie, I know, I really do, how horrible I've been to you and how I was to Hank. You know this is hard for me. I've never been good at … talking … or being a mom. Or a wife. I know. I know that. I always thought I'd get a chance to make it up to you both, but …" Her voice broke, and she had to pause. "I know it may be too late, and I know you will have very strong feelings about what you want to do, but I was up all night thinking about this, and I would very, very much like for you to come live with me. I don't expect everything to be instantly perfect, but I really want us to give it a shot."

Gennie kept her head down, watching the strange hands that held onto her own. She realized that tears were streaming down her face, too. "I-I guess I don't know. I can stay here with Carl. Pat just proposed to me last night, too."

Sylvia's eyes shot to Carl as if for an explanation. Carl just shrugged. She continued, "Oh, baby, you've got a lot of thinking to do," Sylvia said, smiling through her tears and rubbing Gennie's hair. "As a parent, I've got to say you're way too young, and I don't think you should make such an important decision until things calm down a bit, but I would also say I'd love to be around when you do get married."

Carl watched the two women hug and get each other's shoulders wet with their combined tears. Their sobs sounded interchangeable. It was pure crap that this was what brought them together. He looked out his small window toward the track, his lips as tight as his throat muscles, with one tear making its way down his face.

***

The first thing trackers noticed as they arrived for that race day was the headline *Racing Form* story that dealt with their track. It was the story of a fiery mare and how she had thrown and killed her rider after winning the Kensington Mile. What a way to win a race, some thought. What a way to make the front page, thought others.

***

Gennie pulled her baseball cap down low to avoid detection as she entered the track grounds. She didn't want to have to talk to anyone. Not yet. She wasn't ready for a pity party. That could wait for the funeral, now scheduled for Tuesday, a dark day at Kensington, so everyone could come without worrying about missing a race.

Pat met up with Gennie in Rob's barn after the day's last race. He was still dressed in his riding shirt, pants, and boots but without silks. She thought he looked extra nice that day, like a dashing Prince Charming coming to her rescue. She touched the black fabric tied around his arm, and he told her that all the riders had worn black armbands in honor of Hank that day. Then he sat beside her, kissing her forehead and taking her hands. "I got your message. What's up?" he asked.

She studied the face she had already memorized during the past years. Then she had to look away to announce, "Sylvia came over this morning and invited me to move in with her."

Pat's face turned stiff and severe. "What'd she say?"

"She apologized … finally. She actually seemed really concerned about me and said she wanted us to give it a try. Her dad's opening more restaurants in town. She wants to stay here for a while now."

"Oh, and for how long? Until she finds a new guy to take her away and abandon you again? She's full of shit." When Gennie didn't respond to his statement or even meet his eyes, he gripped her hands more tightly and moved his face closer to hers, trying to get her to look at him. "What did you tell her?"

Gennie broke away from his grip and stood up. "I didn't tell her anything yet. I don't know what to do. I mean, Carl can't want me around forever. I could try to get my own apartment back here. But I'm thinking that maybe I should get back in school—I've only got a year left anyway—and it starts up again next month. I don't know. And, really, right now, I don't feel like being here. I couldn't even go trackside today. I don't know when I'll be able to look at that finish line again."

"You know you'll get over that. It'll take some time, but you'll be OK." Pat stood up to meet her and took her hands. "I gave you another option. You could move in with me: I'd like you to. We could get married first to make it official."

"Pat, I mean, geez, I don't want you taking me in out of pity. That's not a real good reason to get married—we both know that."

"For God's sake, you think I'd do that out of pity? I was going to ask you sooner or later: it just happened sooner than we expected." He lowered his voice to a loud whisper as a groom led a horse by.

"I'm only seventeen, Pat. I sure feel older, but I just can't see getting married as a teenager. Can you see the other kids in school calling me 'Mrs. Southgate'? Or me taking my husband to homecoming? I don't think so." She stood against the barn wall and folded her arms across her chest. She studied her still almost-new boots until she had to look to see why Pat wasn't responding. He was sitting down on the bench and staring at his boots. He seemed genuinely solemn. "Pat, I mean, sure, maybe someday we will … but I don't think now's the right time."

"You want to go live with Sylvia, don't you? You want to go and take advantage of her fancy apartment and car and get spoiled because you're afraid." He continued looking at the stable floor. "You're not willing to tough it out. You just let Sylvia sweet-talk you into thinking she'll make everything all better for you, didn't you?" His tone was sharp. But the most astute listener could hear a quiver in his voice.

"Jesus, Pat, I know she's no saint—I'm the first to tell you that. But she is my mom, and I am a kid, and, yeah, Pat, I am scared. I don't want to be left alone. I don't want to be a track rat with no money and no food and no future. If I'm taking advantage of her, it's because she owes it to me for what she put us through." Now she was the one desperately trying to get him to look her in the eyes, but his remained fixed on the ground.

"We could've made it. We're both working here now anyway. You know I'm doing better every season. Rob even suggested I go to Arlington next year. Money would not be a problem." Pat looked toward the track, his jaw locked.

Gennie went and sat beside him. "Jesus, Pat, I need you now more than ever, and you're just turning on me. Sylvia doesn't live that far from here—I mean, this isn't the end of anything if that's what you're thinking."

He finally turned his stony face to her. "You are younger than you think—than I realized, too. So you're right, if you want a mother, go to Sylvia because I'm not going to be a mommy for you. And I'd like to think that nothing will change, but chances are, Gennie, everything will. You want to run away to

Sylvia like she ran away from you when things got tough. I guess it just runs in your family." He turned and gave her a long, gentle kiss that she did not return, and then he stood to walk away. "Do what you have to do."

Gennie watched him walk toward the apartments, but he never looked back. She felt her shoulders begin to tremble and her lips to quiver. She realized she wasn't breathing, and suddenly she had to gasp for air as though she was drowning. Her hands were shaking, and she felt dizzy. Through tears, she saw another groom walking in her direction, so she quickly wiped her eyes and walked the other way.

That had not gone as expected.

***

Gennie had only one suitcase to take. She and Carl had already said goodbye when he left to start his workday. She tried to look around the apartment for anything she might have forgotten, but she didn't have the patience. She walked out of the apartment, closing the door tightly behind her. She walked slowly through the scratched and banged-up beige hall and down the flight of stairs. When she got outside, she stopped to inhale the scents of the track as if to try to get them inside of her. She looked toward the barns and the track, trying to recognize the figures moving in the distance, but they were too far away. No one was running toward her, like in the movies, with one last desperate attempt to make her stay. No one at all.

The black SUV pulled beside her, and she threw her bag into the back seat, carefully setting the bulletin board next to it. She got into the front seat, and this time, she was the one who didn't look back.

So within four days, Gennie's world—and Pat's, and Carl's, and Sylvia's—made a tumultuous turn. You could blame it on shock, the raging hormones of a teenage girl and boy, or most likely a combination of the two. You could blame it on the maternal instincts that manage to creep into even the most unmaternal-like of women. But what's the point of assigning blame? Plots change, and plots thicken, sometimes even without a screenwriter's guidance. Life goes on, friends. Yes, life goes on.

Schooling the Filly

"Mornin'. Welcome back," said a janitor as he did a final sweeping of the front stairs of the old and stately St. Joseph High School. Gennie glanced over her shoulder to see who else was behind her, then realized she was the only student within sight. He had no idea who she was or wasn't; he wasn't even looking up. She responded, "Thank you. Good morning," and trotted up the stairs.

Gennie was about an hour too early for school, but she was still waking up crazy early every day anyway. She left the apartment before Sylvia woke up to avoid the maternal show of "baby's first last day". Gennie had seen her mom's camera sitting on the kitchen table, and there was no way in hell she was going to let her take her photo wearing the stupid new school uniform. Gennie left a note to let her know she'd wanted to get to school early and that she was OK going on her own.

Gennie walked through the empty hallways full of lockers and tried to remember the tour the principal had personally given her the week before. She could already feel the new black flats that Sylvia got her starting to rub against her ankle. She stared down at the red-and-blue plaid skirt, her white legs that hadn't seen daylight in as long as she could remember, and the simple blue polo shirt embroidered with the St. Joseph logo. She had never felt more ridiculous and uncomfortable in her life. She felt like she was auditioning for some porn flick about schoolgirls in need of an education. Too bad she hadn't bought new knee-high socks: that would have been the perfect accessory. She then realized that was what Ruben would say. She felt a smile sneak onto her lips.

Her mother insisted on paying for her to attend St. Joe's, the private school whose students were always at O'Casey's. The irony was not lost on Gennie. Sylvia said it would be better to have one good year of private education to make up for the one she'd missed, but Gennie thought she just wanted to show off that she could afford it now. Gennie and Sylvia had met with the principal and her adviser the week before to review her transcript and discuss the classes she'd have to take to graduate in May. Both administrators promised that none of her teachers would have to know she had skipped a year of school. They both sympathized with her and assured her that she would find St. Joe's a welcoming community that would help improve this most unfortunate situation. Gennie thought of the glares and giggles at O'Casey's that had never seemed too welcoming but still nodded politely. She knew it didn't matter; she would hunker down, get it done and over with. She didn't need to be homecoming queen. She didn't care if she had friends. In fact, she didn't want any friends. She wanted to be alone, if that was possible in an "inclusive learning community of five hundred curious and eager students" like the brochure said.

After a few wrong turns, she found her locker, struggled with the combination, and finally opened it. From her backpack, she pulled three photos from her old bulletin board. One was a *Racing Form* mug shot of Hank. Another was a blurred photo of Carl, Ruben, Rob, and herself at a party at Rob's house. The final one was of Pat, an eight-by-ten-inch winner's circle photo of him aboard some forgotten gelding that the track photographer had given her last year. She taped them carefully on the inside wall of the locker so you couldn't see them unless you put your head inside. She had thought about putting the pictures on her new bedroom wall, as she always had, but she didn't know if she could handle seeing them every day. She thought catching glimpses between classes during school days would be just enough. As she taped her schedule inside the locker door, she heard the sounds of other kids arriving for the first day of school. Giggles and squeals and hugs and high fives and general glee. She slammed her locker door and, with her chin tucked low so she wouldn't make eye contact with anyone, quickly climbed the two flights of stairs to Room 310 for the start of her new routine.

"Oh, good morning! I don't recognize you, so you must be Genuine Harrison," proclaimed her homeroom teacher as she entered. "I know everyone in this school. I'm Mrs. Plinter. Welcome to St. Joe's," she said as she gave Gennie a firm handshake. The teacher looked about her mom's age but a little plumper, with blonde hair and a big smile.

"Thank you," Gennie said shyly, looking around the empty room. "Please just call me Gennie."

"Of course, Gennie." She scribbled a note in the portfolio she was carrying. "Take any seat you'd like. What school did you come from?"

"Delavan High," she answered, choosing not to disclose the missing year since she'd been there. "I've moved in with my mom now, and she thought this would be a better school for me."

"Divorced?" Mrs. Plinter said, nodding compassionately as though she already knew the answer.

"Uh, well yeah, my folks were divorced, but my dad died this summer."

"Oh no," the teacher gasped. "I'm so sorry, dear. Well, we'll make sure you feel at home here. We have all sorts of clubs and activities to get you involved right away. I think that's important for someone in your situation, don't you agree?"

Gennie took a deep breath and slowly released it, shrugging with a tight smile. "Well, I guess I'm willing to try." She slunk into a seat in the second row and started digging around in her backpack to avoid further discussion.

As the other students started filing in, Mrs. Plinter introduced each one to Gennie. Most of them smiled or just nodded as Gennie smiled back nervously. She noticed that her homeroom only had fifteen kids—a far cry from the twenty-five or thirty in her Delavan homeroom. It was a short session: the principal came on over the intercom to make announcements, a student read a "welcome back" prayer, and then the bell rang again, signaling the start of classes.

Gennie grabbed her schedule from her backpack to double-check the room number of her next class as she strategically let all the other kids leave the classroom before her. She was still looking at the folded piece of paper as she stood up and headed for the door when she was startled by a voice beside her.

"Hi, Gennie. Welcome to St. Joe's. I'm Anita," said a bubbly red-haired girl with bright purple glasses. Her hand was extended pretty much right in Gennie's face. Gennie shook it and gave her a weak smile. "Did I see you walking down Sullivan Street? I was behind you a block or two and noticed the uniform. It will be super cool to have someone to walk with now. My BFF's dad is in the army, and they had to move this summer. Doesn't that suck? Right before her senior year, they make her up and move. So sucky. So where do you live?"

"Um, I'm with my mom at the Stanford Towers. My mom just got a place there, and, well, I really need to figure out where I need to go next. Sorry." She looked back at the paper, which Anita snatched from her hand.

"No problem! You've got an official guide to St. Joe's now. Let me help you." She scanned the paper. "Cool. You're right next to my next class. No probs. Let's go." Anita kept Gennie's schedule but whooshed out of the classroom so Gennie had no choice but to follow as Mrs. Plinter said goodbye to both girls.

And so that's essentially how the whole first day went. Even though Anita's classes were mainly AP versions of Gennie's standard ones, they pretty much followed the same pattern, and Anita became her guide all day. By third hour Gennie was expecting Anita to be at her classroom door at the end of class so she could show her where to go next. For lunch, Anita had brought her own vegetarian bagged lunch, but she was still well aware of the hot lunch process and sent Gennie on her way while she saved her a seat at her table.

Despite all the warm and fuzzy brochure copy or big promises from school administration, everyone knows that the real test of a school's true character is always the lunchtime cafeteria. That's where you learn whether the morning politeness was just lip service. It turns out Gennie was treated like a rock star. The lunch ladies recognized she was new and helped her enter her student code in the scanner. The one behind the counter explained what was included in her meal plan. The one at checkout reminded her that she could choose any beverage from the cooler—milk, soda, iced tea!—and most of the kids she passed on her way to Anita's saved spot smiled at her, even if they didn't invite her to join them.

"OK, so this gives us a good overview of the school clans," said Anita from their table against the back wall. Anita sat next to her rather than across the table from her. Only two other kids sat at the far side of their table, and they both seemed immersed in computer games on their laptops. "The table over there is the Brain Trust—the overachievers, the academic elites. They're all nice, and if you ask them to help you understand something from class, you'll have yourself another BFF." Anita pointed to the far-right corner of the cafeteria then scanned left. "Then the one over there are the jocks. Again, actually nice kids, but you better know sports stats to strike up a conversation, you know what I mean? Then we've got the Mosh Pitters. All they care about is music, so you better know the latest indie band if you want to get on their good side. But it's good if one of them gets on the party planning committees because they know the best DJs in town. And … who else … oh, the drama kids. Oh, the drama!" She couldn't help but laugh at her joke. "Again, really nice, but literally overdramatic all—the—time!" Anita threw her hand to her forehead in mock distress. "And there are the debate club kids and, oh, the environmental club! They're some of my friends. I'll introduce you later. They do lots of fun fundraisers and stuff …"

Gennie kept chewing through the whole tour, nodding politely and glancing at the tables to look like she was processing the data, but she thought all the kids looked the same, so she'd never be able to differentiate them anyway. When Anita was finally done and took a bite of her bean and cheese soft taco, Gennie asked, "So where are the mean girls? There's got to be a clique of them at every school, right?"

Anita grinned. "Well, not gonna lie, sure, we have some mean girls. But not many. And they live among all the groups, so they're scattered about. So they're easy to avoid, usually. That's what's kind of cool about here. Most of the groups are pretty OK. Look, at most of the tables, there are even mixed classes. I mean juniors sitting with seniors, look—there's a sophomore sitting at the jock table. If you can find anything in common with them, there's an in. No one's too snooty. Well, maybe the drama kids," she giggled. "But they can't help themselves."

Gennie made another scan of the room while finishing her meal. She did catch a few curious eyes looking her way, but she was always the one to look away first, so she never saw if they smiled or smirked.

"So, do you know where you're going to apply for college yet?" Anita continued. "I want to get into writing. Or film. Maybe journalism. Maybe creative. I'm still trying to figure it out. Maybe broadcasting! That would be cool. There are so many good schools. I need to start narrowing my choices down. How 'bout you?"

Gennie stared at her, finally realizing that a college prep school might be more than she was ready for. "Wow. Yeah, no, I haven't given it much thought, actually. Senior year—such a big deal in itself, right? I just thought I'd get started and then see what happens."

For the first time all day Anita remained silent while she tried to process this information. Then she shook it off. "You're right: plenty of time to figure it out. Most colleges will let you apply all the way up to March. But the ones I'm looking at start taking applications in November, which is pretty much right around the corner!"

Gennie smiled meekly and nodded. "Yeah, I'll have to get serious about that soon. But now, where is Room 01A? That's where I need to go next." Anita automatically jumped back into tour guide mode, and Gennie rescued herself from more uncomfortable questioning.

At the end of the day, Anita was waiting for Gennie after her last class. "Wanna walk home together? We could stop at O'Casey's, this kind of diner place where the kids hang out. I could introduce you—"

Gennie smiled politely, "Aww, that's super nice of you, Anita, but I think this all was enough to digest for one day. I'm just going to head home and maybe get a head start on some of the reading assignments for the week. But you go ahead. Thanks for all your help today." She tried to turn and walk decisively to her locker, but Anita reminded her it was down the other hall.

"OK, no worries," Anita said with a smile. "I'll just show you a shortcut way to walk home."

Gennie could tell immediately that there was no shaking her clingy new friend. As the crush of after-school traffic brushed past her in the hall, she decided having one friend to keep her from all the others would be OK. She even invited Anita into the apartment where her mom was just getting ready to go to the restaurant for the dinner shift.

Sylvia gave Anita an overly enthusiastic welcome with a firm handshake and an offer of milk and freshly bought cookies from the grocery store. "It's so nice that Gennie's already making friends. I was afraid she'd be too cold to talk to anyone." Gennie raised her hands and shot her a warning glare, and Sylvia stopped talking and simply smiled sweetly.

Anita seemed oblivious to the comment as she looked at the assortment of cookies. "This is so fun! Like the first day of kindergarten all over again. New friends AND cookies!"

Gennie rolled her eyes at Sylvia, who shrugged at her while Anita was engrossed in the selection. "Well, Anita," said Sylvia, "I'm sure she didn't tell you, but today is also Gennie's birthday! She said no celebrations were allowed, but I thought cookies certainly don't count as a celebration." Sylvia smiled at Gennie, who glared back.

Anita squealed. "Oh my gosh, that sucks to have a birthday on the first day. I totally would have decorated your locker if I would've known!"

Gennie looked flustered, "No, no—no decorating necessary at all! We just celebrated early instead. Did a little family thing over the long weekend." She shot a look at Sylvia to make sure she wouldn't contradict her fib. "I don't need more than that. But thank you for the sentiment, I appreciate that."

Sylvia surprisingly helped by changing the subject. "Anita, I hope you can help Gennie get involved with some things at school to fill her time with more than just studying. She deserves to have some fun her senior year, too."

"Mom, you know I just want to hunker down and concentrate on school. It's hard enough to figure out all these new teachers and what they expect …" Despite knowing that Sylvia was doing this on purpose, Gennie's glare continued. It seems the mother-daughter acting pair were finding their chemistry.

"But it's your senior year! In my senior year, it was much more about having fun with your friends than stupid ol' books!" Sylvia winked and shook her hips at Anita, which warranted another eye roll from Gennie. She hadn't rolled her eyes in two years, and now she couldn't stop. Gennie was sure that the teenage-girl eye roll would not exist if it weren't for corny mothers.

Anita giggled while sipping her milk and watching the fun interaction between mother and daughter. "Gennie, you're lucky your mom wants you to have fun. Mine doesn't seem to get that aspect of high school at all. And now that the ACTs are done, really, how much do your final grades count, right?"

Sylvia gave Gennie a smug smile. "See, dear, someone appreciates me. But I've gotta go to work." She took both of Anita's hands and added, "We just opened a new restaurant over by the River District—you'll have to come to check it out sometime after school. But for now, stay as long as you'd like. But no boys or beer while I'm gone. Wait until I'm back! Ha! Just kidding. OK, bye-bye now. Nice meeting you, Anita." She gave a dramatic wave and left the apartment.

"I guess she could join the theater kids clique, huh?" Gennie said, finally biting into one of the cookies when the door closed.

"She seems super cool," Anita said. "I wish my mom was fun."

Gennie let those words sink in. Someone was admiring her mom? Gennie didn't even know where her mom was living a year ago. She shook it off and put her school smiles back on. "Well, thanks for all your help today, Anita. I really appreciate it. I'm sure I'd still be searching for my locker if it weren't for you."

"Oh, no worries at all. Tomorrow I can explain the whole B-Day schedule thing. I swear the school does things just to test our cognitive abilities or something," she said while scanning the apartment with her cookie in hand. "Wow, I really like your place, too. So modern. My house feels like a 1970s sitcom."

Gennie looked at the white carpeting, gas fireplace, and funky furniture and smiled. "Thanks. Mom went all out to get something nicer than our last place."

"Well, she did a good job! OK, I'll let you start your reading. Super nice meeting you! I'll wait for you outside your building tomorrow around seven-thirty, OK? See ya!" Anita tossed her oversized, jam-packed backpack over her shoulder and headed out. "Hey, maybe this weekend we could go to the movies. I love movies! Do you know The Times? They show the coolest foreign films!"

Gennie just smiled. "No, I don't, but, yeah, sure, maybe."

"Cool!" Anita smiled with genuine excitement over having a new friend.

Gennie watched her walk down the apartment hall, then closed the door and sighed. She'd survived day one. Maybe she could do this after all.

***

And so went Gennie's first week at St. Joe's. Anyone watching her (and, yes, all those other seniors were watching her, even if they were doing it from a polite distance) would think she was blending in well. Gennie did hunker down with her studies, and she used her study halls to ask teachers questions to ensure she was grasping all the concepts. She was afraid she'd be rusty at learning and studying but, to her surprise, it came back quickly and she actually enjoyed all but her calculus class (would she really ever need to know all that stuff?). Anita dragged her to the annual Involvement Fair, but Gennie would only sign up for the environmental club and intramural volleyball, mainly to shut Sylvia up about "doing things". Sylvia had even asked her if she'd try out for cheerleading. What the hell? Every once in a while, Sylvia's total lack of knowledge about Gennie brought this dream screeching back to reality.

But perhaps the real reason Gennie signed up for some activities wasn't just to appease her mother or to avoid having another annoying conversation with her. Maybe it was so Gennie would have fewer excuses to look at the new phone Sylvia gave her for messages, less time to grab the local paper to check race results, less energy to keep looking at the bus stop near the apartment that she knew would take her right to the entrance of Kensington Downs. Perhaps if she were busy enough, she wouldn't think about Pat's arms around her that last night on the couch; less time to think about her horses watching for her daily approach in the barns; less time to see her father sprawled out, lifeless, on the soft Kensington dirt. Perhaps the more she threw herself into this role, starring in a new sitcom about the down-and-out girl who breaks away into an exciting new land of opportunity, the more she could leave that down-and-out past behind. Just concentrate on acting the part of an average American high school senior. Smile for the school photographer. Feign excitement about going to the local art cinema to see the latest Italian release. Join another club. Go to another meeting. Let the camera follow her from school to home with no hint of longing for anything she left behind. Little did Anita know how well Gennie would have fit in with those drama kids. If she had tried out for the school play, she definitely could have earned the lead.

Bearing Out

Gennie felt the phone vibrate against her shin. She had her back-pack on the floor, leaning against her, with the phone in its little pouch. It was going off, and she could feel it, and it was the middle of social studies class. As motionlessly as possible, so the teacher wouldn't notice while lecturing, she reached into the pouch and turned the phone just enough to see the caller ID. Carl. Her eyes darted to the classroom clock. It was only 2:00 p.m. She had given Carl her new number in case of emergency when Sylvia gave her this phone. In case of emergency. It was the middle of a race day. Carl should be working. What was wrong? Was it a paramedic calling because he found her number programmed into Carl's phone? Had he been crushed in the starting gate? He'd been involved in a couple of accidents already. Or did he witness something? What if it was Pat? Carl wouldn't just call for something not serious.

Gennie's heart started pounding, and she noticed she was breathing deeply through her open mouth. Her hands shook as she tried to set the phone back into the pouch. There were only ten minutes left in the class. Certainly, it could wait ten more minutes, she told herself.

The phone vibrated again, indicating he had left a message. Or someone left a message. Who left the message?

In those ten minutes, she learned what a panic attack felt like. If they were paying attention, the kids sitting near her would have seen how her body was shaking. She slipped on her sweater because she was suddenly freezing. She tried to control her breathing so no one would notice and she wouldn't pass out. She tried to pace her breaths in time with the secondhand that seemed to move ridiculously slowly around the face of the clock. She heard absolutely nothing the teacher said, and when the bell finally rang, it sounded like an explosion.

***

"Hey," she said softly as she peeked into the private hospital room. Pat looked up from reading a *Racing Form* and looked genuinely surprised. He set the paper down and tried to prop himself up more.

"Hey," he replied. "Who … How'd you know?"

She walked over to his bedside. "Carl called me." She handed him a *Sports Illustrated* magazine she had picked up in the hospital gift store. "I brought you something to read in case you're bored."

"Thanks," he said, taking it while studying her somber face, her hair pulled back in its standard ponytail. A few wisps of loose hair hitting her face implied she had either pulled it back in a hurry or it was windy outside. "How are you?" he asked.

She laughed. "I really don't think the bedridden guy in a hospital gown has the right to ask me that. How are you?"

He smiled. "I'm all right. I should get out later today. They just took a few more X-rays to be safe. Once the doctor looks at those, I should be good to go."

Gennie nodded. He looked good, she thought. No tubes in his nose or down his throat, just a wide scrape across his left cheek. It was nearly impossible for his short hair to look less than perfect. She couldn't see what bandages were beyond the bed sheet. Her instincts about the midday phone call had been correct. Pat had been in a spill that had crushed some ribs. Not out of the ordinary for race riders, but it was no fun either.

She sat down on the chair next to the window. "I was still in class when Carl called. It freaked me out pretty good. I thought something … that something more serious might have happened." Despite herself, she felt her eyes well up, and her throat tighten. She looked away to the window as she tried to slow her breathing again.

Pat immediately knew what she was thinking. "Gennie, I've had spills before. You know that. Not every spill …"

"I know not every one," she replied sharply. "But it only takes one, doesn't it?"

He sighed in frustration, then winced at the pain that caused his broken ribs.

"You know," she continued, still looking out the window instead of meeting his eyes, "it was always something that happened to other people. Stories that went around the track kitchen. But now that we're part of one of those stories, I can't stop thinking there will be more. I expect bad news now. I can't stop thinking about that spill. Every night I dream about it. In the middle of a class, suddenly I'll feel it happen all over again. I don't know if I'll ever be able to look at the track again without seeing it." She stared at the hospital carpet, red and purple and blue lines merging.

"It's all part of the game, you know that," Pat said. "What happened to Hank is rare, Gennie; it doesn't happen every day. But spills do happen. I know what to do when I'm falling."

"So did Hank," she replied, still looking down, her throat and face tight.

Pat sighed. "Give it time, Gennie. It's still fresh: it wasn't that long ago."

She wet her lips. "Here's the thing. I don't know that I want to give it time."

He tried to reposition himself again without wincing. He didn't want her to see that. "What do you mean?"

"I mean, I'm not sure I ever want to watch a race again. Every time I do, I just keep waiting for … I don't know. I hate feeling that way and don't want to. I don't want to worry about you and Carl and everyone else every single minute. I don't think I can handle it. Just waiting to call Carl back, I felt like I was having a heart attack. I don't want to live that way. I think I've had enough already. I think I'm done with racing."

Pat didn't know what to say. He knew other riders who had dropped out after witnessing something terrible, but most just got right back up—like you were taught to since you were a kid. "You've been through a lot. You don't have to rush into anything. The change of scenery is probably best for you right now. I get that."

She nodded and could finally look up at him. "You know, I'm not sure where we left things other than it seemed pretty clear you were pissed at me."

He exhaled and studied his sheets. "I know. I'm sorry. I know I just kinda snapped. Pissing you off was the last thing I meant to do, and I did it anyway."

She stared at the carpet pattern again. "You didn't piss me off. You broke my heart."

He looked up again, even though she didn't meet his gaze. "You broke mine first. I guess that's why I lost it. To go one minute thinking, 'This is it, she's the one, let's get married next weekend,' to the next minute with you basically saying you'd rather be as far away from me as possible … It was a bit much to take, I guess."

Gennie nodded, her eyes welling up again. She quickly wiped them with her sleeve and turned to the window. "I didn't mean to hurt you, Pat. I just needed to get away from everything."

"I know," Pat said. "I understand, or at least I think I understand. You don't ever want to see a track again, and I kinda am at the track all the time, so …"

They looked at each other. Neither knew what else to say.

After a few moments of awkward silence, Gennie asked, "How long will you be out?"

"At least four weeks. Rob said I could convalesce at his place."

"Mrs. Wayne will love that. I bet she's already baking you cookies and fluffing up some pillows." She knew that Rob's wife didn't like being an empty nester.

"Yeah, I'm sure you're right. It'll be nice to have some time off. I haven't had a vacation in over a year since I went to see my folks. Hey, maybe you could come by on the weekend and hang out. It's not at the track, so …" When he saw her smile fade, he quickly added, "And bring your homework, of course."

She shook her head. "I don't think so. I can't—I just need to stay focused."

Pat studied her face: her eyes that wouldn't meet his, her lips that refused to smile. "All right. Do what you have to do. I'll be OK. Oh—and just so you don't hear it through the grapevine— when I get back on track, I'm going to head with Rob to Illinois for a couple of weeks. His filly Renegade Sue is doing really well and qualified for a good race up there."

"Wow, that's great. Good luck."

"Thanks."

They met each other's eyes. Both sad. Both happy. Both longing. Both questioning. Both with no answers.

"Well, I better go." Gennie broke the spell as she stood and looked around as if she was afraid she was leaving something behind.

"It's kind of a bummer to think that it took you thinking I was dying for a visit," Pat said quickly while she scanned the room. That made her stop and pause by the window, looking out over the hospital parking lot.

She finally moved over to the bedside and took his right hand. She wanted to say something witty, sarcastic, or sweet, but her mind was racing with mixed signals about what would be appropriate. She smiled, squeezed his hand, and walked away, blinking the tears out of her eyes so he wouldn't see them.

Pat watched her go and stared at the open doorway for a while, expecting her to come back again. But she didn't. He briefly looked down at the magazine, then turned toward the window and stared at the sky until the nurse returned with his discharge papers.

Playing the Field

About a month into the school year, once Gennie was feeling somewhat acclimated to her new surroundings and class schedule, Anita rushed into the early morning cafeteria and dramatically dropped her heavy backpack on the table next to an astutely studying Gennie, nearly startling her senseless.

"What the heck!" Gennie said after being so rudely interrupted from her pre-quiz cram session. But one look at Anita and she knew something was wrong. Anita was the one who looked upset. "What? What's wrong?"

Anita folded her arms, pursed her lips dramatically, and looked up to the heavens while trying to compose herself to speak. After a dramatic pause, she began, "Gennie, I just don't know what to think! I'm the one who showed you the ropes around school. I helped you with intramural volleyball. I got you in with the Greenpeace club, I helped fix your whole socks situation, and now Ray Carr likes you. What the hell?" She put an extra dramatic emphasis on "hell" and then plopped down on the stool next to her. Her long red ponytail, tied with a scrunchie in the school's red and black colors, flipped back and forth with her shaking head.

Gennie's face contorted in confusion. "What on earth are you talking about?"

"Only because Susan told me so this morning, just now, by my locker. She and her pack were hanging out with Sebastian, Steve, and Ray last night and said that Ray asked her all about you. So she was asking me all these questions about you so she could report back, which is crazy because we all know she's been the one crushing on him for like forever, and she's only doing this to get to talk to him more. I tried to be careful with my answers so she couldn't use them against you, but then I thought, why the heck am I trying to help you get on Ray's good side when that's all I could ever dream of …"

"Oh, Anita," Gennie said calmly, "Who's lobbying to join the drama club now? Just because he's asking questions doesn't mean he likes me. It only means I'm the one person in school he doesn't know." Gennie tried to return to cramming for her quiz. Ray Carr was the senior class president, a member of the varsity basketball team, a member of the Key Club, and a popular guy overall at St. Joe's. Gennie had met him briefly at a senior class meeting the week before. Her first impression was that he was nice—not just faking it—and good-looking, she had to admit, but he was part of the high school scene that she avoided. She had no interest in hanging out with him or his other equally good-looking and popular friends. She had Anita; that's all she needed to get by.

Anita finally sat across from Gennie so she could be even closer to her face and whispered sternly, "Do you know what I'd give to know if Ray Carr ever even asked what my name was, let alone if I had a boyfriend?"

Gennie just grinned but didn't give her the satisfaction of looking up. "Well, I'll be sure to sit home and wait for the phone to ring then."

"You don't even care? You're just going to let this opportunity getaway? Could you at least promise to give him my number if he does call you?"

"Well, I can't make that promise …"

"You're impossible!" Anita glared at her.

"Sorry, Anita, I don't need any drama right now. I just want to focus on schoolwork so I can get my diploma in spring and get on with things. I don't need any pretty boys to distract me from my task. I am a master of concentration and focus."

"Right. Like anyone is going to believe that!" Anita thrust her backpack over her should and stormed off as the homeroom bell rang. Gennie found herself smiling as she picked up her books and followed close behind.

So at this point, it does make one curious to know if there had been signs of Ray's attention before poor Anita's discussion with Susan. If you rewound the film and played it back, paying attention to the background characters, you would notice that more than once Ray did walk through volleyball practice, supposedly on his way to shoot hoops, but shooting some glances Gennie's way, too. He never said anything to her but always gave a grin and a nod if they made eye contact in the crowded halls between classes. He had made some early morning cafeteria stops, too, where he might have sat anywhere in the vast sea of empty tables but chose a seat facing Gennie. Coincidence? Perhaps. But that seems unlikely, doesn't it?

***

Gennie couldn't help but think about Anita's entertaining discussion that morning as she entered her life skills class, the only class she had with Ray. His seat was right behind Gennie, and it had been that way from the first day of classes, so it must have been sheer coincidence. But as she entered class this day, it took some effort for her not even to look his way as she sat down. She wondered if he thought she was rude for not at least nodding at him as she usually did. Anita sat in front of her and gave a not-so-subtle raised eyebrow greeting while also looking Ray's way. Gennie shot her a "stop it now" glare, and she sat down as the class began.

It's quite amazing to observe the entire language teenage girls have developed with the eye region of their face, isn't it?

The teacher introduced a new section about personal law and what situations you may find yourself in. After talking about misdemeanors and small claims court, the teacher assigned a small group project where students were given a scenario that they would have to script and play out for the class.

As fate would have it, because fate loves these sorts of things, the teacher assigned students in groups of three based on their seating, so Gennie, Anita, and Ray were assigned to be a team. They were given a speeding ticket case. They were told to script out the defendant's case and how they would present it in court. What would be the plea, and what was the rationale behind it? They pushed their desks together for the last fifteen minutes of class. Gennie finally made eye contact with Ray with a simple, "This will be fun," comment as they rearranged the desks. She wasn't even sure if she was being serious or sarcastic. She found herself talking for the sake of talking. What was with that? Anita immediately volunteered to play the defendant. She smiled broadly as their small group came together to discuss the strategy.

"This will be cool to work on," Anita remarked, her face beaming.

"I think we'll be able to win easily," Ray said. "I've already talked myself out of two speeding tickets."

Anita laughed loudly and asked what type of car he drove. Gennie sighed and looked out the window.

Ray saw Gennie's gaze and quickly said, "I agree. It's too hard to concentrate here. Should we get together tomorrow to go over it instead? I've seen you two in the cafeteria before homeroom; if you want, we could do it then."

"That's OK with me," Gennie said. "We can all read the chapter tonight and be prepared."

"That's a great idea," Anita said. "Our own little breakfast club! Let's say 7:30 a.m. tomorrow?" They all agreed and left the classroom together, Anita waving goodbye to Ray and Gennie shaking her head in embarrassment.

***

Oh, Anita. We've all known someone like her at some point in our lives. Those good-intentioned friends who feel they need to be fate's assistant and help direct emotional traffic in the best interest of their friends. In their defense, they do mean well, but so many things can go wrong when you try to mess with the natural order of things. However, that being said, sometimes those empathetic souls get things right.

That next day, as Gennie walked to school, she realized that it was more than unusual that Anita said she couldn't walk with her today. Something about her mom dropping her off because she had something else to do. Why wouldn't she have invited Gennie to get a lift instead of walking, too? Gennie quickly realized Anita was abandoning her. She had this planned. Gennie sighed out loud and shook her head. Silly, stupid Anita. Why did she have to be so cliché sometimes?

Sure enough, Anita was not at the cafeteria table. But Ray appeared to have been there a while already with books and papers spread out on the table. Gennie quickly scanned the vast room to see if Anita was hiding behind a pillar to watch from a distance—something she'd definitely do—but Gennie couldn't spot her.

"Mornin'," Gennie said as she opened her backpack to retrieve her book. "Anita must be running late. She said something about having to do something with her mom… I'm sure she'll get here soon. Maybe she'll bring us all coffee."

"Oh, you're a coffee drinker?" he asked.

Gennie looked up from her backpack unpacking and looked confused. "Isn't everyone?" When he smiled in reply she noticed his extra white teeth probably hadn't ever been tainted by bean juice. She tightened her lips to avoid showing her less-than-white teeth.

"Oh, Coach tries to keep us on a strict diet. No sugar, no caffeine, that sort of thing."

"Coach. Oh, that's right—basketball, right?" Gennie wasn't sure how much she should reveal that she knew about him already.

"Yeah, the season's starting soon so Coach already has us working out to be in shape when it's go time."

Gennie nodded. "Cool. Um, should we wait for Anita or …" She desperately looked toward the doorway that remained devoid of the nosy little red-haired matchmaker.

"That's OK; I think I got the gist of how she wanted to plead the case," Ray said. "I made an outline last night of how I think we could win it." Gennie was genuinely impressed as he went over it carefully, nodding at some of the notes similar to the ones she had jotted in her notebook. Gennie reviewed her notes, added a few comments that Ray agreed they should add, and scribbled them into his notebook. Every once in a while, Gennie would look at the cafeteria clock and then toward the entrance, but Anita was never there. "Well, I guess this is like the real thing—getting no help from our client," Gennie said as they packed up their notes and books when the homeroom bell rang. "It's not like her to blow people off."

"I'm willing to bet she didn't show up purposely," Ray said matter-of-factly.

Gennie was truly surprised. "Why would you say that?" she asked, making eye contact with him for the first time that morning.

"Because I'm guessing she thought I'd want to use this opportunity to ask you out."

"Oh, God, no," Gennie was shocked that he had gone there. "What? No … I'm sure her mom made her do something. She's always late to—"

"Sorry," he said, cramming his books and notebooks into his backpack. "I didn't mean to offend. I just, I mean, my neighbor Susan … Well, I know she talked to Anita."

Gennie realized she may have overreacted. For the second time in her life, Gennie blushed as she carefully tapped her notebooks into an even stack. "Uh, well, then, this is awkward."

Ray was the one now who wouldn't make eye contact. "Sorry, my bad."

"No, I mean," Gennie scanned the room while looking for words. "I meant I don't think Anita would have been that calculated … Do you? You've known her longer than I have."

He smiled, "She's always been sort of a character, so I'm not too surprised."

"Hmm," Gennie said, staring into her backpack and rearranging some notebooks while holding back a nervous grin.

"Well, I wouldn't want her calculated effort to be for nothing," Ray said with new enthusiasm, "so I might as well try." He smiled, and Gennie noticed his white teeth were also perfectly straight. "So, do you like basketball games? I've got tickets for

Saturday night to see the Bearcats play. It's just a preseason pep rally type of scrimmage thing with another school, but it should be fun. A group of us have tickets. You could meet some more people from here."

"Well, I've never been to a basketball game, but sure, that sounds like fun," Gennie said, biting her lower lip. She at least knew the Bearcats were the local college's team.

"You've never been to a game?" he asked, and Gennie noticed the pitch of his voice went up a bit. He couldn't believe it.

"Well, in grade school, but no, not since then." She found herself feeling like an idiot.

"Well, do you not want to go to a game? I mean, we don't have to—"

Now she realized she got him uncomfortable again. "No, I mean, sure, we can go. It's not that I don't like basketball, it's just that I haven't known anyone else to like it—" She stopped when she saw him staring at her in genuine disbelief. "I'm sorry, let's start over. I'd enjoy going to a basketball game. You might have to remind me of a few rules or something. It's the game with the hoops, right?"

He smiled, relaxing at last. "Yeah, hoops. Sounds good. Should I pick you up?"

"Oh, well, yeah, I guess that's what we should do. Sure." She quickly gave him her address. She was out of breath, and as she tried to put away the notebook and pen, she realized her hands were slightly trembling.

***

What the hell just happened? Stone-cold Gennie, our fierce but broken heroine, just let fate take its course. Well, fate, with a bit of help from Anita's intercession. Interesting. Yes, fate indeed loves to shake things up!

127

Game On

For those who had seen Gennie and Pat together everywhere and at all times at the track, usually holding hands—at the diner, in the stables, in the jocks' lounge, in the upper stands at the end of the day—they might find it surprising that Gennie seemed frazzled over spending a few hours with this other guy. After all, she had already received a marriage proposal, so shouldn't she be an expert on relations with the opposite sex? And yet our heroine suddenly seemed to be acting her age. Even though she and Pat had spent practically every spare minute together at the track, they rarely had gone on a "date". Maybe the first time they'd eaten together at the track's diner was a date, but that was as close as it had gotten. They had gone to the movies now and then, but Carl, other riders, or other grooms always seemed to be with them.

Strangely, it was in scripting in her head how to downplay the event to Sylvia that Gennie found herself listening to her own words and realizing that she should chill.

It wasn't actually a "date". She was joining a group of classmates to hang out at a game. No big deal. No pressure. No expectations.

Yeah, right.

This eighteen-year-old girl turns out to have the same blood and the same nerves as all other teenage girls, and new things were scary. Watching teen movies wasn't going to help her figure out how to handle this: what to wear, what to say, how to act. Was this an act? Did she have to figure something out? Why did it matter? She shouldn't care about what Ray or any of his friends thought of her. But it was nice to be invited out, and she had seen enough movies to know that it wouldn't be fun to be the butt of jokes for the rest of the year. All these thoughts raced through her brain while trying to fall asleep that night. She realized she needed to reach out for some advice, and she knew it couldn't be to Sylvia.

She decided she would have to talk to Anita again after all. After the study group abandonment, Gennie had hoped to give her the cold shoulder for the rest of the week, but when Anita showed up all smiles and giggles at lunch, Gennie decided that she didn't have time for that.

"Fine, Anita. You were right, OK? Ray did invite me to some stupid basketball game this weekend," she admitted, trying to keep a straight face despite Anita grinning ear to ear.

"Oh my God, I don't believe this!" Anita squealed. "I'm taking full credit for your St. Joe's school success, so let's just get that clear right now!"

Gennie shook her head and looked around the cafeteria. "Anita, don't be so goofy. I just, whatever, I don't have experience with this. I mean, do I have to run out and buy a jersey or something to wear, or can I just wear regular clothes?"

Anita stopped smiling and stared at Gennie. "Seriously, Gennie, sometimes it seems like you were just dropped on our planet from somewhere else. You never went to games at Delavan?"

Gennie shook her head. "It just wasn't my scene. I had a job, and if I wasn't studying, I was working. I didn't have time for extracurriculars."

"Wow, that sucks. Well, now you get to make up for lost time! Lucky you. And I get to spend my senior year wishing I was going to games with the hottest guy in school."

"Eew, Anita, don't. He's just nice. He's just showing the new girl around. Now, really, what do you wear to games?"

And so Gennie's real senior high school education officially began.

***

As usual, Gennie had been awake for several hours by the time Sylvia woke up on Saturday morning. In her defense, Sylvia did close the restaurant on Friday nights, so she often wasn't home until one or two in the morning. After she showered off the restaurant smells and had a glass of wine to unwind, it could be 3:00 a.m. before she hit the pillow. This morning she came out in her leopard print pajamas with her eyes still half closed, walked toward Gennie who was doing homework at the kitchen table, kissed the top of her head, and went to the coffee maker where a somewhat old but still hot half pot of coffee was waiting for her.

After pouring in some fat-free creamer, swirling the cup carefully to mix it but not spill it, and then wrapping both hands around her mug, raising it slowly to her nose, taking a deep inhale, and then slowly lowering it to take her first sip—with her eyes fully closed now—she swallowed then exhaled and smiled. "It's so nice to have coffee waiting for me. Thank you, honey. Good morning."

"Morning, Sylvia."

"Whatcha working on so early?"

"Well, I'm trying to finish my homework because I'd like to go to the mall this afternoon," Gennie said, sorting through her paper piles to avoid eye contact with her ever-curious mother.

"The mall? Well, that sounds very out of the ordinary for you. What do you need?"

Gennie exhaled and thought carefully, trying to recall the words she had practiced in her head. "Don't freak out, please, but I'm going to a Bearcats game tonight with some kids from school—"

"Oh my God, are you going on a date?" Sylvia stood tall, eyes wide, coffee cup quickly set on the counter so as to not spill a precious drop should she have to jump up and down.

Gennie looked back down at her paperwork. "Sylvia, I told you not to freak out. I'm just going with some kids from school who have an extra ticket."

Sylvia sat down across from her. "But it's not with Anita. If it were with Anita you'd have said her name by now, but you haven't."

Gennie found herself forcing back a smile, or a laugh, or a grin. How could this woman read her so well when it felt like they barely knew each other?

"Aha," Sylvia said, reading Gennie's mind with that mother-daughter connection that often frustrated daughters. "There is a boy involved. Interesting. OK, there's a $50 bill for the mall if you tell me more." She smiled smugly, and Gennie couldn't resist but take the bait. She'd been hoping for some money by starting the conversation anyway.

"OK, but remain calm, please."

Sylvia nodded obediently.

"His name is Ray, and he might be the most popular guy in the school, but he seems super nice, and I'm sure this is just a pity party to introduce the pathetic new girl to his group of super

131

cool friends. Or maybe it's a big prank, and they're out to make a fool of me on the jumbotron. That's a distinct possibility, too."

To Gennie's surprise, Sylvia just smiled and reached across the table to take Gennie's hands. "Oh, honey, he's not asking you out to make a fool of you. Of course he wants to get to know the beautiful new girl. What guy in that school wouldn't? I'm so glad to see you moving on. I wasn't sure where you and Pat left things."

Gennie's hands darted back at the sound of Pat's name. She quickly went back to re-sorting the homework piles that had already been re-sorted. "Sylvia, it's no big deal, OK. This means nothing. It's just something to do on a Saturday night."

Sylvia just smiled, and Gennie knew that she knew much more than she wanted her to. "OK, sure, honey. We'll go with that. But do you think I should call his parents to make contact?"

"Oh my God!" Gennie said, staring at her. "No! This is no big deal. It's with a group of kids. You don't have to treat me like I'm in middle school."

"Well, is he picking you up?"

"Yes."

"In a car?"

"Of course."

"With other kids?"

"I don't know!"

And Sylvia went on with a hundred more questions for which Gennie didn't have answers. Gennie stared at her, stone-faced and annoyed, as she went on and on. When Sylvia finally paused—probably to think about what she would wear to the wedding in a few short years—Gennie said, "So can I have the money?"

Sylvia looked into Gennie's eyes, searching for some sign that she was her own flesh and blood. When she saw just years of frustration and anger swirling in her daughter's dark eyes, she opened her wallet. Gennie had her as well trained as those mares back in Rob's barn.

***

Gennie found herself unable to eat much dinner on Saturday night. Sylvia had prepared hamburgers and fries, talking away the whole time about her high school days and basketball games. Gennie listened without really hearing, took three bites, and ate a few french fries before she pushed the plate away. She looked out the window without seeing anything. She played with her freshly trimmed hair and adjusted her new sweater. Sylvia finally stopped talking when she saw Gennie's distant look. She was gone again.

"Not hungry, hon?"

Gennie snapped out of it and looked at her. "Oh, no, not really. Sorry."

"You're not nervous, are you, sweetie?"

Gennie shrugged. "I don't think so. I—I don't know. It's stupid, going out like I'm just a normal teenager."

Sylvia stopped cleaning up to come over to the table and smile at her. "But you are a normal teenager. You should be going out with friends on Saturday nights. You are a senior in high school. These should be the best days of your life! I wish I could trade places with you!"

Gennie looked away. "I feel like I'm playing dress up. Like I'm undercover in a witness protection program. I just want to finish school and be done with this."

"My daddy used to say, 'Youth is wasted on the wrong people.' Now I understand what he meant! Just try to relax and have some fun. But just to be safe, I put some extra money in your wallet if you need to call a cab home. You never know—"

As if on cue, the doorbell rang, signaling Ray's arrival. Sylvia squealed, and Gennie buzzed him in. "Sylvia, please calm down."

Gennie opened the apartment door, so he wouldn't have to knock again. He was already walking down the hallway and smiled as soon as he saw her. She couldn't help but smile back. As he approached, she whispered, "Sorry, my mom is being weird and wants to meet you."

"No problem," he grinned.

Sylvia was standing and watching his arrival. Her hands were clasped as though she was holding back from clapping. Gennie said dryly, "Ray, this is my mom, Sylvia. Sylvia, Ray."

"Hello, Ray! So nice to meet you!" Sylvia was grinning from ear to ear. Gennie stared stone-faced at her to signal to turn it down a notch.

"Nice to meet you, Mrs. Harrison. I love your apartment."

"Oh, call me Sylvia, dear. Even Gennie does. And thank you. We've only been here a few months, but we're enjoying it. So I hear you're going to a Bearcats game. How's the team looking this year?"

Gennie was surprised to watch Sylvia and Ray have a full-on conversation about the team and their recent past, and expectations for the upcoming season. Gennie couldn't help but ask, "Sylvia, since when do you know so much about college basketball?"

"Oh, I've gone to a few games in my day," she replied, smiling, and Gennie quickly remembered that Bruce had been a gambler, and must have bet on more than just blackjack.

"Wow, look at that view," Ray said as he admired the view from their balcony. "Nice."

"Well, it's always available for parties," Sylvia said, "as long as they're parties that I'm invited to, too!" She smiled too broadly and put her arm around Gennie, who slinked out of her hold and went to grab her wallet.

"Thanks, Syl," Gennie said. "Should we go?" she asked Ray with a false grin that begged him to leave the apartment quickly.

"All right then, kids, have fun tonight. I wish I could join you, but I have to go to work now. Be home by midnight, OK, Cinderella?"

As the door clicked shut behind them, Ray asked, "Are your folks divorced?"

For the first time, Gennie felt ashamed to answer the question, afraid that his perfect family unit wouldn't approve of a girl without a strong family tree. He would learn early this evening that she was just another trash Delavan High kid. They might not even make it to the game before he changed his mind and left her at home. Then she realized she had no intention of ever meeting his parents or caring what they thought about her family. "Yes, they were divorced, but my father died last year, so I moved in with Sylvia."

"Whoa, sorry, wow! That's a lot. That sucks." Gennie just shrugged. "But, wait, before … you lived with your dad?" he continued. "Like full custody? Isn't that unusual, I mean, for a divorce settlement?"

Gennie laughed, then decided she couldn't possibly explain a mother who initially, and correctly, thought a failing jockey father would be a better parent than herself. "My dad was great. I loved living with him. And besides, Mom moved to another state, and we didn't want to disrupt too much of my life, you know, at one time." She was proud of herself for providing such a believable fib. "How 'bout you? Let me guess: two great working parents, a couple of siblings, and a yellow Labrador retriever at home, right?"

He smiled as he let her exit the elevator first. "Well, no. Not at all. Except for the Lab—Buddy. And he's a chocolate Lab. Sorry if I was rude asking all those questions. But maybe you could give me some advice. My parents are going through a divorce right now. It's kinda ugly. And it's making my mom go a little bit crazy, which is why I think Dad's place might be a calmer place to crash, but I wasn't sure they'd even allow something like that in the courts, which is crazy to even think about because I'm almost eighteen anyway. But I also don't want to push my mom over the edge, so … Yeah, I'm glad you accepted tonight to get me away from it for a while."

Gennie was surprised. She didn't expect the school's most popular hero to have anything other than a perfect origin story. "Oh, I'm sorry. I know it's tough. Well, actually, with my folks, I was kind of glad it happened, and it happened quickly."

"I never saw it coming," he said as he opened the car door for her. She thanked him and remembered how Pat opened and closed doors for her every time. She always wondered where Pat had learned manners like that. He was so young when he moved out on his own. She shook her head discreetly to shake clear the thoughts of the past. "Nice car," she said because she couldn't think of anything else to say.

"I feel a little guilty about it because I know Dad was just trying to prove he's a great guy by giving it to me before he moved out."

"He's got me believing," Gennie said, and Ray laughed.

When they got to the game, several other kids from school were in their row. Anita had been right. They were a group of season ticket holders. Gennie could only imagine how much their parents paid for the center-court seats. She wondered why Ray had an extra seat. Whose spot was she replacing? Ray introduced Gennie to all of them, and she smiled but said little.

The game started with a dramatic team introduction in a darkened arena with loud music and courtside cheerleaders trying to work the crowd into a frenzy. They seemed to do their job well. Gennie kept her eyes on all the action but was well aware of the group of kids next to her sharing years of familiarity and inside jokes, and common backstories with each other. Gennie would turn and smile politely when they all would laugh at some shared memory.

She tried to focus on the game instead of what she was missing from their personal conversations. She applauded when Ray did and scowled when the guys swore at the refs. She was amazed at the height of the players and laughed internally at the extreme differences from the last crowd she hung around with. Ray wasn't grossly tall like some of his friends, maybe not even six feet, but he was still the tallest guy she had been around in years. She was used to being the tallest in the room in her old life. Then she caught herself. Her old life was her life. This, whatever it was, was not. She was doing what she needed to be doing.

She watched the game clock and wondered if there was an intermission. She looked around at the other people to see if she knew anyone, and of course, she did not. Ray whispered in her ear, "Are you OK?"

She was surprised. "Yeah, of course, I'm fine."

"Really?" he asked, and she noticed he had very nice brown eyes. "You look like you're looking for an escape exit."

"No, I'm just trying to understand it all."

He then proceeded to whisper the general rules and regulations of the game to her so as not to embarrass her in front of his friends. She noticed that his whispering in her ear caused a weird tingle in her spine. The two other girls in their group noticed the extensive amount of whispering between them and started to whisper to each other about what they might be discussing. Gennie thanked Ray for enlightening her and offered to buy him a soda as a thank you gesture as a time-out was called. He went to the concessions area with her but refused to let her pay. She raised a toast to him, thanking him for helping a basketball-challenged idiot try to fit in. "My pleasure," he said, giving her another perfect smile that she tried to ignore.

After the game, his friends suggested that they go to O'Casey's. Ray looked at Gennie with disappointment. "I'm really sorry, but I've got to get to a preseason open gym practice tomorrow morning at eight. Would you mind not going to O'Casey's, or—"

"Oh, that's fine," Gennie said with relief. "I've got a pretty full day tomorrow too," she lied.

Gennie realized then that maybe he was backing out of O'Casey's because he wasn't having a good time with her and just wanted to go home. Perhaps he was bummed at having to teach her every little thing about his favorite sport. Or, maybe there was another girl that would be at O'Casey's, and he didn't want to be seen with Gennie. She suddenly felt awkward and—surprisingly—a little disappointed. She felt the urge to talk to Anita.

What? Where were these thoughts coming from? What did she care?

They drove back to Gennie's apartment in near silence as she took a keen interest in the sights passing by her window. When they pulled up to her apartment building, Ray switched off the ignition and got out quickly. Great, he can't wait to get rid of me, she thought as she trudged out, only to be surprised when he rushed over to open the door for her. "Oh," she said, embarrassed, "you surprised me."

"Mademoiselle, après vous," he said, extending an arm toward the building door.

"French," she said. "Impressive."

"Ha! Just freshman year, so I could learn enough to impress the chicks," he said, and she laughed.

He escorted her into the elevator and pushed floor number five, then quickly four, three, and two. "What are you doing?" she asked, concerned and confused.

"Trying to buy more time," he said, and she instantly blushed. Ray grinned and looked around the tiny box of a room as the door opened at floor two. "I had a good time tonight," he said.

"Thanks for being patient with me. I know you probably think I'm an idiot," she said.

"Not at all. You're a quick learner. You know, maybe, tomorrow after practice, we could go to O'Casey's for a late breakfast, if you want."

She found herself smiling despite herself as the door opened for floor number three. "Well, I have a paper to write, but I do have to eat breakfast sometime, so I might as well... Sure, what time?"

"Meet me there at ten-thirty?"

"Sure, sounds good," she said, then waited awkwardly, biting her lip and looking at the elevator carpet pattern as the door opened at the fourth floor and then slowly closed before proceeding up to their final destination.

Ray smiled as the doors finally opened for the fifth floor.

They walked in silence down the hall to her door. Gennie's brain was racing with what to do next. There was no way she was inviting him in. Why did he even bother coming into the building? Why didn't they stay in the car to talk about O'Casey's?

Ray cleared his throat. "You know, if you don't kiss good night on the first opportunity, then every opportunity after keeps getting tougher because then you wonder if you've waited too long, or if it's a good time, or maybe you should wait until the absolutely perfect next opportunity …"

Gennie's eyes went wide as she looked for her apartment key in her pocket. "You sound as though you speak from a lot of experience," she said, avoiding eye contact.

"Nah, it's what I've been told," he said.

Barely thinking, she reached up and gave him a little kiss. "Thanks. It was fun. I'll see you tomorrow."

Gennie didn't even wait to look at his reaction. She quickly let herself into the apartment, closing the door softly behind her. The doors were soundproof enough that she couldn't hear if he turned and walked away immediately or if he stood there soaking it in (which, by the way, is precisely what he did—a neighbor leaving to let his dog out for the night saw him).

Gennie stood there, leaning back into the door and feeling her face flush over. She could still feel her lips on his lips. She could still see his surprised brown eyes. Her whole body began to tremble, and she thought she might be sick. She took a few deep breaths and walked to her room. She noticed Sylvia had left a lamp on before leaving for work, but she still wasn't home. Gennie crawled into her bed without washing her face or brushing her teeth. She lay there with her eyes wide open, staring at the white ceiling above her and using it as a screen for a mental old home movies projection show: first, of the track, and Hank, and Carl, and Pat … then Sylvia, smiling and laughing, and tonight Ray, with that gentle little grin as he explained basketball rules quietly into her ear. That tingling sensation that shot down her spine. Gennie clenched her eyes shut, but the images kept coming. It was like she knew she was starring in a movie, but she didn't have the script. There was no way of knowing where this was going.

A Change of Pace

"Anita, calm down," Gennie said firmly over the phone. It was Saturday afternoon, and she was returning Anita's call from hours earlier when Sylvia had answered and told her that Gennie and Ray were already out on their second date. Sylvia and Anita had a good old-fashioned girls' giggle fest over the new pairing. Now that Anita had Gennie's ear she was going on and on about how she was mad that Gennie hadn't called before going to O'Casey's. "Anita, listen. I'll tell you everything because there's not much to tell! Yes, he's as nice as you said he was. That's all, OK? I barely talked to his friends, but they were all cool. I mean, I didn't feel like they were being snarky or anything."

"Oh my gosh," Anita gushed. "Did you make out?"

"Anita! Oh my God. No. Stop. Not interested." Anita couldn't see Gennie's grin on the other side of the phone, but Sylvia could as she snuck glances while flipping through her fashion magazine at her daughter talking on the phone at the kitchen table. Gennie finally ended the conversation by saying she had to finish her paper. She looked up to see Sylvia grinning at her from the couch. "You stop, too!" Gennie said, then turned back to her stack of textbooks, the grin still on her face.

If anyone had been keeping track of the days that Gennie had smiled in the past three months, it wouldn't have been hard to do. The kids at school saw her as always looking serious. The apartment building neighbors in the elevator would describe her as always quiet but polite. The teachers assumed she was shy. Her mother saw her as always looking lost. But none of them would say she looked happy except, maybe, for right now.

***

That week Ray smiled at Gennie each time they passed in the hall, and he joined her and Anita for lunch several times. On Thursday morning, he surprised her before class by rushing to sit across from her while she reviewed some notes for a quiz. "Wow, what's the hurry?" she asked.

"I wanted to talk to you before Anita gets here," he said, looking around. "Sorry, no offense. But one of the guys on the team is having a party Saturday night. I thought maybe that would be a good way for you to get to know more kids around here. Wanna come?"

She started putting her notes back into her backpack. "I don't know. Parties aren't really my thing. I never remember names, and you have to mingle and talk to people ... and I don't know."

"Yeah, sounds like torture," he said sarcastically. "C'mon, Gennie, it'll be fun. I'll introduce you to everyone. If it's not fun, we can always leave."

Her mind was racing. She had assumed he'd ask her out again, but she hoped it would be to do something less intimidating than hanging out with his fan club.

"Thanks for the invite, but I'm really not much of a partier. I'm the straight and narrow type."

"The kid hosting is a varsity athlete. He's not going to risk his status for a party. It'll be mostly clean."

"Mostly?"

He smiled and cocked his head. "Yes."

Ray looked at her with his brown eyes, and she couldn't say no. "Fine, but I can't stay late. I've got another paper to finish this weekend." Anita showed up, and Ray smiled and darted off.

"Oh my God, did he ask you out again?" she asked.

"Yeah, to some stupid party. I'm already dreading it."

"Oh my God, is it Tony's? On Saturday? I would KILL for an invitation to that," Anita said dreamily. "Maybe I can chaperone you two?"

Gennie just sighed and shook her head.

"That's fine," Anita continued. "There's a Fellini Film Festival at The Times that I'm going to. Alone. But whatever."

"I'm sorry, Anita. I'll go with you to the next one, promise." Gennie smiled apologetically at her and they both went to homeroom. Gennie spent most of her day wondering about the party and if she could dream up a good enough excuse to skip it.

On Saturday, Ray showed up right on time again, wearing a long-sleeved Henley shirt with the school logo on it and a pair of khakis, the unofficial school uniform of the guys of St. Joe's. Anita, insisting on being her fashion coordinator for the party, had taken Gennie shopping that morning. She talked Gennie into a cute, dark blue striped cardigan over a tight pink T-shirt and some straight jeans with a new pair of ballet flats. Gennie realized that together they would look like those couples at O'Casey's she used to look at. But now she was part of the picture. She felt a little queasy.

This time, Sylvia had already gone to the restaurant before Ray arrived, but she had left Gennie with a strict set of rules for the night: She must leave if there was drinking or drugs at the party; she must leave if anyone suggested strip poker or other inappropriate games; she must call or text Sylvia if she ever felt uncomfortable with Ray; and she must be home by midnight. Gennie almost played the "you know I'm eighteen, right?" card on her, but she knew that she would have followed all those guidelines as an excuse to get out of it anyway, so she skipped it.

During the car ride, Ray tried to brief her on the crowd that would be there, but her mind was racing too fast to absorb anything he said. He noticed her silence. "If you really don't want to do this, we don't have to," he said. "Last week, I took you to a basketball game that you couldn't care less about, and now it looks like I'm taking you to the Colosseum to feed you to the lions."

"That's the analogy I was looking for!" Gennie proclaimed excitedly as he pulled in front of a house lined with parked empty cars. "I wasn't sure what I was feeling. You nailed it."

"Seriously, Gennie, if this is too uncomfortable, we don't have to do it."

Gennie could tell he meant it. "No, no, it's OK. I'll give it the ol' St. Joe's try. I guess I've got to get to know everyone sooner or later."

"Yeah, there's the party spirit," he said dryly.

She could see his somber face even in the dark car. "I'm sorry," she sighed. "I don't mean to kill your Saturday night. Thanks for inviting me. Let's do this."

He grinned. "You sure?"

"Sure." She forced a smile and opened her door.

As they approached the grand two-story home, they could hear music coming from inside. Despite ringing the doorbell twice, no one came to answer. Ray tried the doorknob, which was unlocked, so they entered on their own. Just as they did, a tall guy came sliding down the banister with his legs up. "Hey, Ray!" the guy said as he slid off right in front of them.

145

"Gennie, this is our host for the evening, Tony. Tony, this is Gennie Harrison."

"Oh, yeah, the new girl. Cool. Hi. Come on in. Everyone's in the basement." He took off down the stairs taking about three stairs at a time.

Gennie gave Ray a startled look after the rambunctious host left them. Ray took her left hand. "C'mon," he said, "it'll be OK." She looked at his hand holding hers, then began to follow him down the stairs.

The fancy finished basement was packed with faces Gennie recognized from the halls and classes of St. Joe's. Most people smiled and said hi to her; a few went out of their way to introduce themselves. She noticed a few clusters of girls who just looked at her as they walked by. She whispered in Ray's ear, "Is now a good time to ask Tony if his parents are home? Sylvia told me to ask."

Ray gave her a "don't be ridiculous" scowl and went to the cooler, where Gennie was glad to see lots of power drinks and sodas but no beer. She accepted a Coke from Ray and started drinking while looking around the elaborate basement rec room. Music was blaring from a sophisticated sound system, and a few kids had carved out a corner of the room to dance in. At one point, a guy got dizzy from his exaggerated dance moves and stumbled into Gennie, spilling her soda onto the new cardigan and pink shirt.

She quickly searched for a bathroom to find a towel to dry off, but she was further humiliated when she walked in on a couple making out who had forgotten to lock the door.

She backed out and decided to go upstairs for some paper towels in the kitchen. When she approached the kitchen, she heard a bunch of girls talking: "All I know is that she came from, like, Delavan High."

"Isn't that the public school with all the stoners?"

"That's what I thought. I wonder if her mom had to take her out because she has a problem. I mean, who transfers for their senior year?"

Gennie stopped abruptly and took a deep breath. She started to look for a powder room on the first floor when she turned right into Ray.

"Hey, can I help?" he asked.

"Help get me out of this nightmare?" she asked more harshly than she intended to.

Just then, the group of girls from the kitchen walked by, staring at the two of them and then at each other with surprised eyes wide open. They hadn't expected the target of their discussion to be so close. Ray caught their glances and watched them until they were out of earshot. He turned to Gennie. "Of all the people to ignore at Joe's," he said, "those girls are at the top of the list. What did they say to you?"

"They didn't say anything TO me at all. I've got to get a towel or something. The kitchen must be safe now." She went back to the kitchen to search for a paper towel. Ray followed behind.

"You said you like coffee, right?" he asked after watching her blot her shirt with the paper towel.

"No way am I going to drink coffee here so that can be spilled on me, too," she answered, still working at her stain. Even she could hear the bitterness in her voice.

"No, not here. Let's get out of here. There's this cool new café downtown by the river. We could go there instead."

She sighed. "That sounds great, but I didn't mean to ruin your night out with friends. We can stay a little longer if you want. It just got off to a rough start. We can try again."

"They won't even notice we left. C'mon, quick before they see us!" He grabbed her hand again and darted with her out the front door and to his car without passing anyone else. Once inside the car, he locked the doors and breathed an exaggerated sigh of relief.

She smiled and was glad to watch the party house fade into the distance as they drove away but still said, "I'm sorry, Ray. I didn't mean to be a drag. We can go back if you want. I think my shirt is drying off ..."

Ray quickly glanced over at her with a grin. "You're a terrible liar. There's nothing in the world you want to do less than go back to that party. That's all right. I've wanted to check out this café, so this is great."

She looked out her window and smiled. He could already read her thoughts.

"Do you hang out downtown much?" he asked as they approached the city lights.

"Never," she said. "I'm pretty much an outskirts girl. How 'bout you?"

"My dad works downtown, so we're here a lot. I'll show you the sights."

"Great," she replied. As they drove down the city streets, he pointed out his dad's office building, the little restaurant where his dad frequently went for lunch, and a park with a good hot dog vendor in the summer. They drove out of the business area into a neighborhood that seemed more industrial but bustling, with hipsters heading into clubs and tattoo parlors. He found street parking right in front of the café and could parallel park easily into a spot. It was a refurbished warehouse with exposed brick walls and techno music. The menu of hot drinks was more extensive than her mom's restaurant dinner menu. Ray stood in front of the counter studying the options while Gennie went right up to the clerk and asked for a large black coffee.

"Well, I was going to order a half-caf double moo-moo mochaccino, but fine, I'll take a black coffee, too—but leave room for cream, please," he added and pulled out his wallet to pay for both of them. He added two frosted mocha chip sea salt caramel brownies to the tab, and they headed through the crowd of café tables to find an empty one in the corner. They negotiated the course without a single spill and toasted their success.

Once safely in their chairs, they were able to recap the party and talk about who was who, which led to talk of who else had parents going through a divorce and led Ray to tell Gennie more about his parents. She kept asking him questions to keep the conversation from turning toward her own story. He was open about the tension at home, the fights, the tears, and his mixed emotions. When the last drops of coffee and brownie crumbs were gone, Ray suggested they go out to check out the riverfront.

They paused to admire the boats and the lights across the river. "Ever go to Kentucky?" he asked.

Gennie smiled. "Yeah, probably more than downtown, but mostly when I was a little girl," she said, remembering her family's many trips to breeding farms and Keeneland Race Track and Churchill Downs, but not volunteering those details.

A small pathway ran along the water with a few benches along the way. The October sky was clear, with a perfect view of the quarter moon and stars galore. The air was seasonally crisp. Ray saw Gennie put her arms around herself and took the opportunity to put his arm around her. "Cold?" he asked.

She shrugged. "Yeah, a bit," she said. He pulled her in tighter, and she didn't resist. She was cold. But what was she doing? This tall guy she had just met was close to her. So close to her. She shouldn't be doing this. Why was she doing this?

They walked down the path until it dead-ended into a barricade, blocking the way to a construction site. They stood behind it, admiring the illuminated cranes.

"My dad will probably buy one of these condos. This might be my home away from home one day," Ray said.

"That would be pretty cool to have a place down here," Gennie said.

Ray shrugged. "Hey, thanks for listening to all my personal crap. I feel like I'm a downer this evening."

"No, really, it's OK. It's good to talk about all that. It's good for me, too, to know I'm not the only one who has to go through all that. I can see the kids at the party weren't really into sharing deep thoughts."

Ray pulled her toward him and kissed her. It wasn't one of their quick goodbye kisses like after the game or the diner. This time it was a real one. At first, Gennie didn't resist. He felt good. And warm. And it was such a pretty night. And, damn it, she was a teenager in high school. Then she giggled.

"What?" he asked, backing up and looking for what might have happened.

She covered her mouth, ashamed and embarrassed but still choking back a giggle. "Oh, God, I'm sorry. I-I have coffee breath—"

Ray looked at her like she was crazy. "We both do," he said.

"Right." She laughed, looking back to the river and trying to figure out what she was doing. The smile wouldn't leave her face. The giggling kept coming. What was happening here?

Ray tugged at her hand. "I'm sorry. Did I do something I shouldn't have? Should we get you home to Sylvia before I try anything else?"

She looked at his friendly brown eyes that literally were sparkling under the streetlights, took a deep breath, and giggled again. She let out a frustrated groan between giggles. "I'm so sorry, Ray. I normally don't giggle. Really." She tried hard to swallow the last of her outburst. "I guess I'm just kinda surprised by all this."

"I'm sorry, I shouldn't have—"

"No, no. It's OK. Which is what's so funny." She stopped, realizing he saw nothing funny at the moment. "Ray, I—I just never thought that I would be out having fun with some tall, handsome guy from St. Joe's."

He cocked his head with a smile. "OK, now that's sounding better," he said.

"Look, I didn't want to come to school here. My mom coerced me into it. I thought it was a school full of stuck-up snobs. So I guess I just wanted to do my time in heavy resentment and then get out. I never dreamed I'd actually have a good time during this last year."

"And is it awful if you manage to fit some fun into your otherwise grim and resentful life?"

"I just realized that, no, it's not," she said, smiling at him. He looked at her, unsure of what to do next. She reached up, put her arms around his neck, and resumed the kiss. And finally, the giggles stopped.

***

As the weather became more consistently crisp and the leaves shed their annual display of colors, the rumor mill at St. Joe's was working overtime with news of Ray dating the new girl, Gennie-Somebody, that transfer from Delavan. Glances were shot her way in crowded hallways, through the bustling cafeteria, and in classrooms. There were whispers and even some laughter. Some disbelief, some curiosity, some resentment. High school at its finest.

Gennie walked through it all in hazy focus. Despite her attempts to be invisible, she suddenly realized that although everything around her was blurry, she was crystal clear.

The following week Ray came over to do homework, as was the new norm, but Gennie couldn't concentrate.

"Ray, this may sound strange, but when we went to that first basketball game, I had no idea that you were like school royalty or something."

"Shut up," he said, shaking his head but smiling.

"No. Really. Everyone knows you, everyone seems to like you, and now everyone stares at me like I'm some bad guy who moves into town and steals their hero. I-I don't like the attention, and I had no idea what I was getting into. People stare at me and whisper when I walk by. It's weird; it's stupid."

Ray shrugged. "Our high school is probably dumber than most. Just ignore it."

"I even had to drop out of intramural volleyball because the girls got too freaked out when you showed up at the games."

"Shut up. That's a lie."

"It is not. They actually asked me to tell you not to come because they were too distracted and worried about looking stupid. That was so insane I just walked out."

"They were joking. Maybe they just wanted you off the team. I've seen your serve …"

She threw a pillow at him. "Thanks a lot, jerk. They can have you."

He took her in his arms. "I don't want them. Just you."

"I'm serious. I can't just ignore it," she said, pulling away. "I like being nobody. I like being invisible. I wasn't made for the popular set. I think that maybe—"

"Whoa. Stop," Ray said, suddenly getting her gist. "Don't you dare break up with me on the night I was working up the courage to ask you to homecoming."

"Homecoming! See, this is what I'm talking about. Homecoming is for popular girls who get all dressed up and giggle and act stupid and … Ray, geez, that's just not me."

"Exactly, Gennie. That's why I want to go with you. And, besides, you do giggle. I've heard you."

Despite herself, she felt a strange sensation in her throat—or was it her chest?—and realized she was smiling.

***

Sylvia cheered and did a little dance when Gennie told her about Ray's invitation. Gennie wanted to be disgusted by her giddiness, but she couldn't help smiling as Sylvia went on and on about the preparations that would need to start immediately. "Get Anita on the phone," she instructed like a drill sergeant. "She certainly knows more about this than I do. We have to get this right."

Anita was over in a flash, and after the initial disappointment that Ray hadn't changed his allegiance to her, she let herself be happy for her new friend. With Sylvia, Anita made a to-do list of all the necessary preparations: buy a dress, order a boutonniere, make a hair appointment, go to the makeup counter at the mall to buy Gennie the essentials, buy shoes, get a mani-pedi, and finally get those eyebrows waxed. Gennie just sat at the kitchen table with her homework, shaking her head and listening as her date was planned.

The Big Dance

Anita was over by noon on the day of the dance. She and Sylvia immediately started working out the timeline details to ensure both girls would be ready to go by 4:00 p.m. when the group was meeting for photos. One of Ray's friends, Sebastian, who was also without a date, had asked Anita to go to HoCo at the last minute, which ended up nicely rounding out the group of friends who would take photos together and then go out together for dinner.

Gennie obediently stayed in her room, listening to Anita and Sylvia go on and on about the timeline. She could hear them laughing and high-fiving each other. Gennie let her mind go back to when all her mom did was scream at her dad and do next to nothing for the family. Sylvia was definitely making up for lost time these past three months. It sounded like she and Anita were lifelong friends. Suddenly Anita dramatically jumped inside Gennie's doorway. Gennie couldn't help but smile.

"Gennie! Girlfriend! Time to shake that tail feather! We're going to have our nails done first because we have no idea how long that mani-pedi will take. No offense, but it looks like you haven't had one for a while … and your eyebrows, sorry, but … yeah. And then we'll end with our up-dos … and then maybe grab a coffee if there's time …"

Anita joyfully rattled off the list of to-dos for the day as Gennie put her pillow over her head in protest. "Anita, your unbridled enthusiasm drives me crazy sometimes," she groaned.

As Anita and Gennie sat in side-by-side chairs for their manicures, Gennie couldn't help but think of *The Wizard of Oz* when the unlikely team of trail mates got to Oz and the city treated all of them to makeovers before meeting Oz himself. If they could make that lion look handsome, they can do something with me, she thought as she kept apologizing to the girl working hard to transform her stable-hardened hands and fingers into something pretty. When she was done, Gennie stared at her new smooth hands—now topped with sparkly transparent white polish—as though they were someone else's. She couldn't believe her hands could look pretty, but they did.

Then another stylist took her hair and brushed and twisted and flipped and pinned and sprayed it until her formerly simple, straight auburn hair looked shiny and full and put up into a style like something out of one of the magazines sitting in the waiting area. Yet another woman took on her eyebrows, waxing then yanking, then waxing again, and yanking again until her eyebrows were trimmed and neatly shaped. Gennie grimaced with her eyes closed and tearing up until it was over, then smiled apologetically to the crew who had worked so hard to transform her. Gennie paid for both girls' afternoon extravaganza with a gift card that Sylvia had purchased in advance.

After grabbing some to-go coffees and stopping at the flower shop to pick up the boutonnieres, the girls returned to the apartment, and Anita started on Gennie's makeup. "Not too much," Gennie said. "I feel ridiculous enough already!"

"We're just giving you some sparkle and a little sizzle," Anita said, preparing makeup brushes, tubes, trays, and many other things from a pouch Gennie had never seen before.

"I don't need sizzle," Gennie said, "I need a tranquilizer."

Then Sylvia brought the dress out in a mock ceremony while humming "Pomp and Circumstance." "Mom! I'm going to a dance, not graduation, for God's sake!" Gennie snarled.

"Oh, I know, I know, but what else do you sing? 'Celebration'? OK. Celebrate good times; come on!" Both girls looked at each other and sighed, then laughed as Sylvia continued running around the apartment, singing every old dance song she could think of.

The dress that Gennie had chosen, with careful assistance from Sylvia and Anita, was a shimmery ice blue color with a halter strap that gently wrapped around her neck. It hugged her body and then slowly flowed outward below her hips as it reached her ankles. The shoes had been decided by Anita: silver strappy things with open toes and high heels that made Gennie very nervous. Anita couldn't believe that Gennie had never worn any heels before, so they held several practice sessions to ensure she wouldn't look like a horse walking in them. Gennie had chuckled at Anita's comparison—if only she knew how right she was.

Gennie then tried her best to help Anita get ready, too, but for the most part, she seemed to be more in the way than helpful. Gennie even had a hard time closing a necklace clasp. She realized her hands were trembling.

They were nearly finished when the doorbell rang. Gennie rushed out of her room to try and get to the door before Sylvia, but she caught a glimpse of herself in the hallway's full-length mirror and stopped dead. She didn't even recognize the reflection. She stood there, with her well-glossed lips wide open, studying the stranger in the mirror. "Anita, what have you done?" she whispered. In the back of her mind, she heard a recording of her voice saying, "Can you see me taking my husband to homecoming?" She had to choke back a sudden surge of emotion from deep within her. Both her eyes swelled with tears, threatening to ruin her makeup. She felt light-headed and sick, but then others entered her reflection, startling her awake from the sudden trance. Anita and Sylvia once again high-fived each other on their successful transformation of Gennie's appearance (weren't their hands getting sore by now?), and Ray just stared. Gennie spun around to face him. "This is ridiculous, Ray. Really, why don't you go and—"

But then he broke into his irresistible smile and said, "You look stunning."

Gennie looked back at herself in the mirror. "Oh, I don't think it's even me anymore."

"Yes, yes, it is," he said and handed her a wrist corsage, perfectly coordinated to match the dress, purchased undoubtedly with Anita and Sylvia's help.

"And look at you," Gennie said, touching Ray's new black suit. "My God, you could be a CEO in this thing. It's sharp." Ray just smiled as Anita swooned behind him.

Gennie tried to pin on Ray's boutonniere, but her hands were shaking badly so Sylvia stepped in to help. Sylvia snapped about fifty photos, and then the three kids went to Anita's house to meet her date.

The four of them then went to a local park to meet the other kids and posed for dozens of photos in front of a small army of parents. Gennie smiled politely and complimented the other girls' dresses as the other lifelong friends hugged and giggled and shouted to each other to come over for small group photos. She tried to lean forward onto her toes to avoid her heels digging into the ground. Anita was trying to blend in and act as if she had always been part of this group. Gennie noticed that the only person in this clattering herd quieter than herself was Sylvia, who stayed silently on the sidelines as the other parents, who had also known each other for years, were chatting away. This seemed to be the adult equivalent of O'Casey's. It wasn't until Ray's mom, her eyes red from crying while watching the kids enjoy such a happy day, found Sylvia to introduce herself. Gennie kept an eye on the whole exchange and thought Sylvia looked nervous. Interesting. Ray came to grab her for a small group shot with some of his very besties (not to be mistaken for the broader group of just regular besties), where he gushed to her, "I've known these guys since 4K!" She smiled and nodded hello to them, then posed according to parental instructions with the other dates. After twenty minutes of this, she felt she had her homecoming smile perfected.

Gennie once again looked for Sylvia, just in time to see her walking to her car. In an instant, she was sprinting (as fast as her heels would allow, that is) toward her. "Sylvia!" she yelled, then, "Mom!"

Sylvia stopped and turned with a surprised look on her face. "Hey," Gennie said, "don't go before we get a photo together."

Gennie immediately turned back to find Anita to take the photo. Anyone who might have been watching Sylvia's face would have seen a transformation from a little bit awkward, sad, and uncomfortable to the proudest beaming mom in the universe. Anyone who studied the resulting photo, if they zoomed in, would see a bit of moisture in that formerly hard and cold woman's eyes.

Ray then took a photo of Gennie, Anita, and Sylvia. The smiles in that one showed laughter and joy.

The kids then sent their parents packing and headed to Sylvia's restaurant for a discounted homecoming special meal deal. Although Sylvia came in later as a manager, she kept her promise not to interrupt them and embarrass Gennie. But she did spend a lot of time observing the group from a safe distance and pointing out her beautiful daughter and her handsome date to any of her workers who happened to pass by.

After they realized they were already late, the boisterous party broke back into their small groups to drive to the transformed gymnasium, where everyone already there stopped and stared as they entered. Many kids thought Ray had brought someone new to the dance, not recognizing Gennie. Gennie walked carefully and kept her eyes down, studying the flooring pattern with every step. "You've got to relax if you're going to have any fun," Ray whispered to her.

"I'm not trying to have fun," she replied, looking around at all the other sparkly gowns and high heels. "I'm just trying not to fall."

"Yes, you want to have fun, and I do, too." She smiled at him and nodded in agreement. She pledged to herself that she wouldn't be a Debbie Downer for him tonight.

"Hey, Ray?" she asked, and he leaned in to close her ear. "Yeah?"

"Did you ask Sebastian to ask Anita to homecoming?"

He flinched back as if offended. But then came back to talk into her ear so she could hear him above the loud music. "Why would I ever do a thing like that?"

Gennie tried to ignore that back tingling sensation she got again from him talking so closely into her ear and replied, "Because you knew how heartbroken she would have been to miss her senior homecoming?"

When she looked to him for his answer, he shrugged and threw up his arms. "Homecoming Karma, I guess." But the glimmer in his eyes told Gennie all she needed to know. Damn, he was a nice guy.

"Dance time!" Anita yelled as she appeared out of nowhere as if on cue and grabbed both of their hands, pulling them to the dance floor.

"Uh, Gennie?" Ray whispered as he was pulled along.

"Yes?"

"I should have told you this earlier, but I'm not a good dancer. At all. Really."

She looked back to see that Ray looked nervous now.

"I've never danced in my life," she admitted to him. "So I guess we can suck together."

They both laughed as each began dancing more awkwardly than the other. Anita and her date watched in horror at their awfulness and moved away to dance with others who were taking it more seriously. Gennie found herself laughing so hard her throat hurt. Then the DJ suddenly switched the tone of the dance to a slow song, and Gennie automatically started walking back to the sidelines.

Ray grabbed her hand and pulled her back. Their eyes met, and the laughter was gone. "Can we try a slow one?" he asked. "I doubt even we could screw that up."

At that moment, she recognized the song. It was some new band's hip version of the old Sinatra song "The Way You Look Tonight". Oh, Daddy. Was he here somehow, watching over the festivities? She smiled and blinked away tears before Ray would see them and moved quickly into the closer stance, feeling comfortable and pretty, wrapped in his arms, and for the first time, not minding if the other kids stared at her.

We know fairy tales are fiction. We know movie and novel romances are fiction. We know that most of what we perceive as reality is fiction. But that doesn't stop us from loving it or buying into it with our hearts and souls. Why not? Why not escape reality for a while to believe that backtrack girls with hands calloused from a life of actual labor can be made up all pretty to dance with a prince, if even for just one night? Why not let ourselves go and be entertained until we're forced back to our realities?

Benchwarmers

And so our starlet was finally comfortable in the spotlight. The small-town girl plucked from obscurity and accidentally given the lead role in a production that even the drama club couldn't have dreamed up was finding her groove on the set. She wasn't memorizing any lines or giving any autographs yet, but she was finding her way around the script and making it her own. She was marking it up, redlining parts that we'd assume would happen, and penciling in new directions to keep us on our toes. She was still just living day to day, putting the priority on her schoolwork and her few extracurricular activities. She was letting Ray ride along, like one of those stable ponies or goats that trainers sometimes brought in as buddies for their high-strung steeds.

No, sorry. That's going too far.

Ray was more than a stable pony, but that might be one thing Gennie wasn't quite acknowledging yet. She did indeed enjoy his company and their discussions about family life. She'd never had someone to talk to about unhappy parents. She was enjoying her role as supporter-in-chief of Ray's misery at home. She sincerely did want to help him through it. And, though she probably wasn't ready to admit it, she looked forward to giving him advice. Anyone just tuning in might think that she was his stable pony. She was helping keep him calm through his senior year storm. So, you see, they were helping each other more than the other could—or did—know.

***

The Saturday after homecoming, Gennie woke up late. She was surprised to see the clock read 9:26 a.m. She hadn't slept that late in years, perhaps ever, in her whole life. She was always up by dawn to take care of somebody or something. She let the thought cross her mind that she was changing. Her attitude was changing. Her outlook was changing. And then she quickly jumped out of bed, shook those uncomfortable thoughts from her head, slipped on the souvenir homecoming sweatshirt they all got last weekend and went to the kitchen to make herself breakfast. Sylvia's door was still closed. She had closed again last night, and she had no problem sleeping late to recuperate.

Gennie started the coffee maker, poured herself a bowl of cereal, and flipped on the small kitchen TV to find something to watch. The first thing she saw was a commercial for the Breeders' Cup races. Gennie froze, spoon halfway to her mouth, milk dripping off.

Breeders' Cup Day. It was Gennie's favorite Saturday of the year. A full day of horse racing broadcast live with back stories on all the trainers, jockeys, and horses competing in the annual championship races to prove who deserved the year-end titles. It was the racing world's version of the Academy Awards, only it lasted all day, and the horses were competing to win the categories right there. Kensington would always have the races broadcast throughout their grounds so the locals could keep up with what was happening on the national stage and bettors could wager on horses and jockeys who would never come to a small-time track like Kensington. The Kensington crew would gather in the diner after the last race of the day and watch the Classic together, then celebrate well into the evening.

Gennie wasn't sure she could even watch it this year. Did she want to? Could she? Would she be sick to her stomach watching it, afraid every second for the horses and riders in the races? She realized she was OK. She did want to watch it. She'd have it on in the background, she rationalized, so that would help keep it in perspective. She had a big paper due Monday; that would be her focus. She knew Ray had basketball practice in the morning and then was working at the hardware store all afternoon. Plus, he had the same paper due Monday so she would not be hearing from him today.

She got her papers, books, and notecards on the table and made a second pot of coffee in preparation for sitting in front of the TV for several hours, watching the eight races televised live. Oh, yeah, and working on that paper.

Sylvia shuffled out of her room around eleven and saw what was on the TV. She considered suggesting turning it off so the two of them could go to the mall together—like a normal mother and daughter—but the intent concentration on Gennie's face was a look that Sylvia recognized and had hoped had gone away with her new life here. Still, she knew better than to disturb her. That girl could be intense.

Sylvia left for work before the races were over, leaving Gennie alone for the night. Since Gennie had spent most of the day with her eyes glued on the TV instead of doing the homework laid out neatly in front of her, she knew she should get serious about finishing the paper, but after the Breeders' Cup Classic champion trophy was awarded, she found herself staring at her phone and the clock. She finally grabbed the phone and punched in Carl's number. Maybe they were all going out together tonight, and she could get caught up … It was a Breeders'

Cup Day tradition for everyone to go out that night. Why not? She could handle it. She wanted to handle it. The phone rang and rang, then went to voice mail. She hung up quickly, shook her head as if to shake the idea out of her brain, turned off the television, and hunkered down on the paper.

**

Gennie had just dozed off, still sitting at the small dining room table over her dozens of notecards, when a loud noise made her jump out of the chair. She thought she had just dreamed it and looked at her watch to see that it was only eight o'clock. Then she heard the noise again. The doorbell buzzer. She panicked, thinking it might be Ray. Did she forget about some plans they had made? She tried to think of what she forgot when the doorbell rang again, this time a long, extended buzz as someone kept a solid push going. Ray wouldn't do that. Anita wouldn't do that. She got a little tense.

She cautiously pushed the intercom button. "Hello?" she asked.

She felt a tinge of fear as she heard several male voices until she recognized Carl's voice among them. "Gennie? Gennie? We're here to visit," said Carl. His speech was slurred, and she quickly realized the tradition of going out had continued. She pushed the admission buzzer and then had to push it a second time as they buzzed back because they all didn't get through the unlocked door in time. Who was here? She listened at the door to hear the elevator stop. She swung the door open excitedly and watched in amazement as the old crowd poured in: Carl, Ruben, Rob's top groom Harry, John, an assistant starter. And Pat. And they all appeared to be phenomenally drunk.

"Gennie, baby!" Carl squealed as he gave her a bear hug. "We miss you, girl! We've all come to visit!"

Pat was next and gave her a warm but silent hug, avoiding making eye contact.

Ruben shimmied up to her in his typical showman style and extended his arms for a hug, but she pushed him away with a laugh.

Harry and John nodded and smiled, then went out on the deck to oooh and aaah at the view, then found their way to the TV remote and surfed the cable channels until they found a station showing old *Baywatch* reruns. John had a near-empty bottle of beer in one hand.

"Well, this is quite a surprise," she said. "I was actually thinking of you guys. I got to watch the Breeders' Cup all day."

Pat was at the dining room table, looking at her notes. "Doing homework on a Saturday night? Quite impressive."

"Quite pathetic, if you ask me," Carl said, coming over to look at the table.

Gennie ignored Carl and looked at Pat, who still wouldn't look her in the eyes. "Not really. It's due Monday; I put it off too long—" As she started to stack the notes up so her visitors wouldn't mess them up, Gennie noticed that even Pat looked a little green. He went and sat on the couch next to Harry and John. She wondered if he had asked to come along or if they had forced him. He had never drunk in her presence before. He wouldn't risk the fines or penalties if caught underage drinking.

"It's Saturday night, girl!" Carl mumbled. "A high school girl should be partying with all her cheerleader friends. I hoped they would all be over here tonight so we could meet 'em."

"I don't know any cheerleaders. Sorry."

Carl moaned and rolled backward on the couch, landing on Harry's lap. Harry pushed him onto the floor.

Gennie looked at her watch. "How did you guys have time to get so trashed this early?" The last race of the day usually went until at least 5:30 p.m., so that didn't leave much time for partying.

"In honor of the Breeders' Cup being in California, the bar had Margarita Happy Hour tonight," Carl said with a smug smile. "Didn't have enough money for food and drinks, so we had to stick to drinks." Gennie's phone rang on the coffee table next to Carl and he instinctually picked it up.

"Allo?" he slurred. "Yeah? Yeah. Gennie? Yeah. Gennie!" he hollered, even though she was right next to him. She grabbed the phone, angry that he answered. What if it was Ray? She startled herself. Wait, why would she care if it was Ray? Why did she care what he might think?

Before she could even say hello, she heard Anita screaming on the other end of the line, "You're having a party and didn't invite me? I can't believe this. I thought I was the only frigging friend you had at school, but now that you have Ray and his friends, you forget about ME!"

"Anita, Anita!" she hollered back until she stopped her screams. "Calm down. I have not deserted you, and I'm not having a party! These are just some very old and very drunk relatives and friends of mine who surprised me with a visit."

"Anita, Anita—couldn't be sweeter," sang Ruben in the background.

Anita changed her tone immediately. "Any cute ones?" she asked timidly.

"Hey, Ruben," Gennie called, "want a girlfriend?"

"Oh, yeah, baby. But no punkers and no preppies—is that what they call 'em?—and two eyebrows. Not one eyebrow, like my Aunt Maria. No, gotta have two eyebrows."

"Anita, you meet Ruben's strict criteria for a girlfriend. Oh, wait, he just passed out, sorry."

Ruben curled up next to Carl on the floor and quickly started snoring.

"How old are those guys? How many are there? My God, Gennie!" Anita moaned. "Ugh, I wanted help with my math, and now I can't come over there!"

"Oh, sure you can; they'll all be gone or passed out soon. Come on over." As she hung up, all five guys were in various states of repose. She smiled, looking at all of them, glad they were there, despite their condition. She was relieved that they were finally quiet so she wouldn't have to talk to them about anything. She just watched them all and felt a feeling of peace she hadn't had in months. Gennie wasn't sure why she had so willingly invited Anita over. How would she explain a roomful of height-challenged drunken guys? She realized she wanted Anita to see part of her old life, but she wasn't ready to explain it all yet.

Gennie let her eyes shift over to where Pat was leaning against the couch. His eyes, half-open, were glued to the TV showing two girls running into the water. He didn't turn her way. Gennie looked back to her pile of homework and wondered what she should say to him if anything. Should she ask him to her room so they could talk things out? Should she just be happy he made this appearance? Maybe it was a sign of something? She was glad he saw her at home alone on a Saturday night doing schoolwork. What if they had tried coming over the night before when no one was home? What if they had caught Sylvia, and she would have told them Gennie was out on a date? Gennie's throat felt like it had sunk to her stomach. But what did it matter? Even if she said anything to Pat now, she doubted he would remember it in the morning. This didn't seem like the time to share any deep thoughts.

Anita arrived in about twenty minutes after having taken some time to apply a touch of makeup and put her hair up. As she entered, Ruben sat up and smiled. "I knew you wouldn't let us down," he said to Gennie with an uneven grin. The other guys stirred and began mumbling. Carl howled with his eyes still closed.

"Sorry, Anita, but they're coming back to life. Let's go in my room and work. You guys, I don't know what you're doing, but if you're staying, be quiet."

Once in her room, Anita began grilling Gennie about who they were, but Gennie just said it was her cousin Carl with his friends whom she hadn't seen in a while. Gennie tried her best to turn the subject into homework. Once they finally got to the math assignment, there was a lazy knock on the bedroom door. "Come in," Gennie said hesitantly.

Pat swaggered in and meandered to sit closely next to Gennie on the bed. "Hi," he said bluntly, and even that made her heart leap. She could feel his thigh snug against her own.

"Hi," she replied and tried to continue helping Anita with a math problem.

"Whatcha doin'?" he asked.

"Some math problems," she answered, not looking at him.

"Oh, I like math," he said, feigning excitement.

"You do not," she said.

"Oh, yeah, you're right. I don't like it at all unless it's in terms of odds in my favor." He stared at the open book. Anita stared at him and then at Gennie, tilting her head and raising her eyebrows, looking for an explanation. Gennie just shook her head. Pat continued, "Carl wants to know when your jackass mom is coming home cuz he don't want to see her."

"Tell Carl she's not a jackass anymore and that she could be home any minute. I don't like drunks, Pat," Gennie said.

169

"Well, neither do I!" he exclaimed, suddenly animated. "Did you see Ruben out there? He's actin' like an idiot, that guy," he said as he lost his balance even while sitting, nearly slipping off the edge of the bed.

"How are your ribs?" she asked. "All healed up properly?"

"You bet. I don't feel a thing anymore." He patted his chest and smiled at her with a glaze in his eyes.

"Why don't you all just go home and sleep this off, and we'll have a real visit some other time?" Gennie suggested.

"Well, we can't cuz we forgot where we parked the car," he replied honestly.

"Well, that's a good thing. I think the bus or a taxi would be better for you at this point anyway."

"That's a very educated thing to say. This school thing is working for you. You're very right. We should all go call a taxi right now." He remained seated.

"Well," Gennie said, "aren't you going?"

"Oh, yeah, I forgot," he said and slowly ambled to the door. He paused, turned to look at Gennie again, and then headed out into the living room. Gennie called a taxi from inside her room and apologized to Anita that she needed to take a break to help her other guests leave. The thought that some of them might start getting sick wasn't appealing.

"The taxi will be here in five minutes. You'll have to squeeze in, but you can do it," she instructed as she piled them into the elevator while confiscating another beer bottle and already thinking of explanations she could make to Sylvia as to why the bottles were in their garbage. "You didn't have money for dinner—do you have money for the driver?" she asked Carl. He dug into his pocket and pulled out a crushed ten-dollar bill. "That should do it," she said. "Don't lose it!" As the elevator door closed, she heard Ruben trying to persuade the others to

170

go salsa dancing. She smiled, imagining what Pat might look like trying to dance, and then she hoped there wouldn't be too many girls at the salsa club looking for cute, inebriated guys to take advantage of. She sighed deeply to shake off the thought and then walked back to Anita, who was waiting to continue drilling her on who all of them were.

"That Pat guy, now he wasn't bad at all, and I think he may like you, but since you've got Ray, maybe you could give me a chance—"

"Don't even think of it," Gennie said. "He's not your type. I mean, you saw him. He's a drunk; he's trouble. He just happens to have a prettier face than the rest of them," she explained quickly while spraying the living room with air freshener. "Carl needs to find a calmer bunch of friends."

Before the inquisition could continue, Sylvia returned home, and Anita quickly exited, vowing that she was going home to finish her math work finally.

Sylvia looked at her watch. "Geez, when I was your age, homework was the last thing I'd be doing this late on a Saturday night!" Anita smiled and shrugged, and exited with a quick "Good night."

As soon as the door closed, Gennie told Sylvia, "OK, don't freak out. I had some visitors tonight. Carl and some of the other guys came over to say hi in honor of Breeders' Cup Day. They were all pretty drunk and—" Gennie stopped when she saw Sylvia's face transform. It took a moment to figure out the expression, but then it struck her: Sylvia looked terrified. The color drained from her face, her eyes were wide like a horse being confronted with a car for the first time, and it appeared she had stopped breathing. All this because her track friends had come for a visit?

"Jesus, Sylvia, it was nothing. They were here for maybe thirty minutes. Anita was here doing homework. I didn't let them puke on anything, but some beer bottles are in the garbage, so I wanted to let you know they weren't from me or Anita."

Sylvia's shoulders relaxed, and her tight lips formed a small smile. "Oh, that's OK, honey. Thanks for telling me. How are the guys?"

"Well, not gonna lie, they were pretty wasted, so I'm not sure how any of them are doing. But they were funny."

Sylvia searched Gennie's expression for clues. "Was Pat with them?"

Gennie quickly started tidying her homework piles. "Yeah, he was and, surprisingly, he was drunk, too."

Sylvia watched Gennie busy herself and knew she didn't want to talk anymore. She never spoke about Pat, or anything from the past, really. Sylvia nodded even though Gennie wasn't looking at her. "OK, then, I'm glad they didn't trash anything. I'm turning in. Good night."

Gennie slowed her tidying when Sylvia left the room. Yeah, what about Pat? She could still feel his thigh tight against hers while they sat on her bed. What did he think of her now? Was she old news, and he was moving on with his life? After their last discussion at the hospital, she sort of felt like they made up, or at least they apologized for that last fight, but he had never texted or called—but then neither had she. And she still couldn't see herself going back to the track. She never wanted to see another spill as long as she lived. She had found herself saying a prayer before each of the Breeders' Cup races and then giving thanks when each race ended safely. Maybe this St. Joe's experience was getting to her. Gennie needed to stay away from horse racing. She knew she had gone back to school to get away from the track more than to graduate. Pat was the track. She could never watch him race down that stretch again. Just thinking about it made her heart start to pound. What would he have said to her if he hadn't been drinking tonight? Or, maybe, if he hadn't been drinking, he wouldn't have come. Even if he was tipsy, he could have said something, anything. But he did sit next to her. Close enough that his denim-clad thigh was pressed against hers. If he had never wanted to see her again, he could have remained standing at the doorway, talking from a distance. But he didn't. He sat next to her, closely next to her.

What if Ray, by chance had called in the middle of all of this? He supposedly was at home tonight doing homework, too. Would he have thought she had been hiding that she was just another party girl from Delavan High with a stable of guys to hang out and party with? He might get afraid of catching some disease from her if he thought that. As the final notecard was stacked up into a neat pile, she told herself she didn't care what Ray thought of her. Or Anita. Or even Pat. She made decisions for herself right now. It was all she could do and what she would do from now on.

Full Court Press

Sylvia plopped the laundry basket onto Gennie's bed. Gennie was at the library, or that diner, or someplace with Ray again. It was hard to keep up. That girl was always doing something with Ray. It was nice to see Gennie get involved with such a cute and popular boy and still get good grades.

There was a stack of schoolbooks on Gennie's dresser alongside a tray with a modest selection of makeup, most of which was purchased for homecoming. Sylvia made a mental note that they should go to the mall for a proper makeover one day. She'd treat Gennie to a whole face's worth of good makeup. That would be nice.

Since Gennie wasn't there to shoo her away, Sylvia let herself take a look around the rest of the room. The walls were bare except for that dumb, dirty horseshoe from the old apartment. On her nightstand, Sylvia found a program from a school play, some ticket stubs from basketball games and movies she didn't recognize the names of (Anita must've made her see them), and a St. Joe's flier about an upcoming meeting for seniors. There was a photo of Hank in a simple wooden frame. It was a closeup. He was smiling and not in racing silks. Where would he have been smiling when it wasn't in a winner's circle? She sat down on the bed to hold the photo and study it. She couldn't remember where it was taken or when it was from. His face was already weathered—she always had told him to wear sunscreen, but he wouldn't listen to her—so he must have already been in his thirties. Even through the frame glass, Sylvia could see the sparkle in his eyes. There was something about the way he would grin at you. Those eyes would grab you, and … She quickly put the frame back, trying to carefully place it in the exact right spot so Gennie wouldn't be able to tell she'd been in there snooping.

She scanned the room one more time, relieved to see a space of a regular teenage girl. Gennie must be at least content here. She must be glad she was back in school, and—Sylvia exhaled slowly—hopefully happy living here with her. Sylvia wished they could talk—really talk—but she realized her place in Gennie's pack and let it go. She was lucky the girl even spoke to her after what a bitch she'd been. Sylvia grabbed a St. Joe's sweatshirt from the floor to add to her next laundry load and scurried out of the room. As it always was with Sylvia, she thought it best to live in the moment and not think about the past or even, sometimes, the future.

***

A brisk wind swirled around the stables as Carl and Pat finished their morning routines and headed back toward the dorms. In the parking lot, a car pulled up, and a girl got out. Carl watched Pat look at her intensely and then turn away.

"It's not her," Carl said flatly.

Pat looked at him, acting like he didn't know whom Carl was talking about, but in one instant, he knew that Carl saw right through him. "It never is," answered Pat.

"You think she'll just show up one day?"

Pat looked toward the parking lot and the main street that led out toward town. "Yeah, I do. But I've been wrong so far. I can't blame her if she's happy with what she's doing. She should finish up school. I get that. But I thought it might drive her crazy, going from being so independent and all."

"I thought she'd still come by on weekends, at least," Carl said.

"No, no, that doesn't surprise me. She's all or nothing. Only win bets—no place or show. I want to think that she's afraid that if she came back, she'd stay."

"Hmm. That's a good way to look at it, even if it'd be because we'd kidnap her and make her stay. I kind of miss her coffee in the morning." Carl stopped to pick up a crumpled Styrofoam coffee cup. "I saw her yesterday, you know."

Pat stopped walking and looked at him. "You did?"

Carl kept walking, and Pat quickly caught up. Carl threw the cup into a wastebasket against the stable wall. "Well, just from a distance. I was walking with Lisa—that new exercise rider—to O'Casey's, and she was leaving with some tall guy with a nice car. Shit." Carl looked sideways to see Pat's reaction. Pat just kept his head straight up and didn't flinch.

"Did she see you?" he asked.

"Nah, and I didn't call out. I didn't want to embarrass her. But Lisa didn't know about Gennie, so I spent our whole first date telling her about 'er, but I don't think she minded."

"That's good. So you and Lisa might work out?"

"Yeah, well, she's nice, I don't know, we'll see. How 'bout you? Lots of girlies in the stands betting on you. I even heard Kelsey Jones talking about you the other day. She'd be a hell of a date."

Pat shrugged. "I guess I should, but, you know, it's been kind of busy and everything."

"Yeah, it's been kinda busy," Carl answered, and they walked the rest of the way to the apartment building in silence.

***

"Merry Christmas," he said.

Gennie looked at the necklace resting in the small box and felt her throat stiffen. It was a small golden horseshoe charm on a delicate sparkling chain.

"I liked it because it seems like you brought me good luck this year, you know, horseshoes and good luck and all," he explained.

She nodded and smiled. Quietly, she said, "It's even facing up. So many people hang them upside down, but then the luck falls out. You must have it facing up to hold the luck in." Her voice broke, and she embraced him. She felt tears. At first, they just seemed like tears of happiness, but then she found herself catching her breath. Her shoulders seemed to quiver, and she realized she was sobbing. Ray stared at her, trying to understand the reaction, but she was unable to speak, unable to understand it herself. So he just hugged her tight.

***

And so ended Gennie's tumultuous, confusing, and complicated year. Of course, no one at school knew that she was at St. Joe's to escape the nightmare of watching her beloved but stubborn father being trampled to death and lying like a rag doll in the dirt. Of course, no one knew that her mother had once abandoned her for over a year. Of course, no one knew she had been attached at the hip to another guy before coming here. Almost engaged. No one knew that just one year ago, she was a broke dropout living on ramen in a slum-like apartment.

They didn't have to. They didn't need to. Sometimes, as Sylvia has taught us, it's better to concentrate on the present.

You Miss Every Shot You Don't Take

By March, Gennie considered herself an expert on boys' basketball. She knew the difference between a two-point and a three-point shot, she understood the difference between a guard and a forward, she got pretty good at spotting fouls, and she knew all the corny school cheerleading chants by heart. She and Anita went to all the home games to cheer Ray and his team on. They hardly needed the support. The team was 12–1 going into the state division three championships.

Ray had given Gennie a complete wardrobe of St. Joe Crusaders sweatshirts and even sweatpants, which she dutifully wore to each game, along with her Christmas necklace. Anita would frequently take it a step further with team-color headbands, and once she even wore face paint, which Gennie made her promise never to do again.

Gennie enjoyed watching the competition and couldn't help but be reminded of watching the stretch runs of thousands of races. The cheering, the heart-pounding excitement, the sheer joy on fans' faces. The wire to wire warrior, holding off challengers all the way to the end. The closer coming from behind in the last yards of a race to win by a nose. The underdog beating the big dogs.

The main difference, of course, was that a basketball game lasted over an hour, while a horse race would be done in about two minutes. But the games inevitably came down to the last two minutes, so there was always an exciting finish. Oh, and, of course, the players were much, much taller.

Gennie and Anita even made the two-hour pilgrimage in Anita's parents' car to watch the state championship game. They both ooohed and aaahed as they entered the vast arena. Gennie got to see Ray just before he headed into warm-ups. He gave her a warm kiss and thanked her for coming all the way to Columbus. "You're my good luck charm, you know," he said, noticing that she was wearing his necklace.

She laughed. "Chances are, I'm not. I think your teammates would be pretty upset to hear you talk so crazy. You guys have worked hard for this. You deserve to be here."

He smiled at her. "Remember when you didn't even know what a three-pointer was? Like, what, just a few months ago? Now look at you!"

She couldn't help but laugh, decked out as she was in her red and black Crusaders ensemble, giant Ray-head poster in hand. "I can't believe you turned me into this," she said, shaking her head—and the cardboard one.

"Oh, so it's all my fault?" he teased.

"You don't think I'd do this for just anyone, do you?" she asked with a teasing scowl.

"You better not." He stole another quick kiss. "Well, here we go. At least wish me luck."

Then she quickly reached up to kiss him again, this time a slow, lingering kiss. "OK, let that be your good luck charm."

The buzzer whistle sounded from the court, and Ray just looked at her and smiled, biting his bottom lip and sighing.

"Yeah, OK." And he jogged off to join the guys. Gennie, smiling, watched him go, then headed to her seat beside Anita and all the other students.

The Crusaders had a rocky start—Gennie blamed it on the refs but, honestly, it might have been Ray's distraction by that kiss—but they rallied to come back so that they were only down by two at the halftime buzzer. The coach must have had a good locker room speech because the guys came back in the second half to take control for a solid ten-point victory and another state championship to add to the trophy case. The St. Joe's fans stayed in the stands, singing their school song, with their arms around each other's shoulders, and Gennie singing loudest of all—totally unashamed and loving it.

***

Later that evening, Gennie's doorbell buzzed. Ray had finally returned from Columbus. "I'm not sure I want to let in someone who can't even manage to get MVP in one little game," she teased over the intercom.

"Let me up, and I'll make it up to you," he shot right back.

She buzzed him in and waited by the door, knowing he would fly up the three flights of stairs faster than the elevator would travel. She was right. He flew in the door for another congratulatory embrace.

"So where's the rest of the team?" she asked when he wouldn't let go.

"Probably O'Casey's," he answered into her hair.

"Don't you want to go?" she mumbled into his shoulder.

"Nah, I had enough male bonding on the bus home."

"So now you've come home for some female bonding?" She said, finally breaking his hold.

He laughed. "Yeah, I guess I did, sorry."

Gennie started analyzing the game and questioning Ray about specific calls that she didn't understand, but he seemed distracted and looked around the apartment. "What's with you?" she asked.

He shook his head. "Is your mom home?" he asked.

"No, she's closing tonight."

He walked back over to Gennie and took her hands. "Gen, I-I don't know how to bring this up." She suddenly felt nervous. He sighed while gathering his thoughts. "That kiss right before the game—that kiss." Gennie caught on and suddenly backed away. He looked at the floor. "Well, it made me think that maybe we're ready to take this relationship to the next step. You know …" his voice faded as he put his hands back onto her waist.

"You're not talking about giving me your class ring, are you?" she said but knew he wasn't looking for humor right now.

"I'm just … I don't know … I wouldn't even suggest this if I wasn't serious, you know. And with the game—Wow! What a perfect day to—"

Gennie broke away again and headed directly to one of the armchairs, where she knew he couldn't follow. "I hate to be a downer on your big day, but that's just not going to happen." She looked out the window at the meager skyline, avoiding his eyes.

"We could be extra careful," he said, sitting on the couch. "Practically no risk at all."

She still wouldn't look at him. "Ray, don't get me wrong, you make it very tempting, but I'm not into taking chances that way. What my parents did to me—I mean, they had me too young. They didn't know what they were getting into, and, well, they messed up. Mom and Dad always fighting—and I had to deal

181

with stuff—well, it made me promise myself that I would never, ever, put a kid into that situation."

"I'm not talking about having kids, Gen," he said.

"I'm talking about accidentally having kids," she said harshly. "I'm not going to take a chance that could mess up a kid's life. It's not worth it. I'm not going to play the odds game over something that important. When I do it, it will be because I'm ready for everything that comes with it. I will not budge on this." She stared at the window, refusing to look at him.

He was silent for a while, then moved over to her chair to sit on the edge next to her. It was only then that he saw the tear sliding down her cheek. "It's OK," he said. "I guess I'm in the same boat as you. I kind of hate my parents for having me right now."

She finally looked him in the eyes. "Don't say it that way. I mean, they didn't know they would end up this way. I guess there's always that possibility, but I'm not going to tempt that fate right now—in high school. We've got enough to deal with, don't we?"

He leaned onto her shoulder and sighed. "You're right. Of course. I just got a little … excited, I guess."

"Well, I mean, who can blame you?" she said, giving him a grin.

"Dang, I miss two MVPs in one day. This sucks," he said, sliding to the floor next to the chair. Gennie reached down and rubbed his shoulders.

"Yeah, it sucks being you."

He sighed and rubbed his temples. Gennie turned on the TV and took Ray's hand to relocate to the couch, and they watched the story of the school's championship on the local news snugly together. When it was over, he decided he'd have to go home and face the congratulations from his mother, who was probably angry that he hadn't been home yet. The two kissed, looked into each other's eyes, and said goodbye. Gennie watched him walk down the hall, and once he disappeared into the stairwell, she closed the door.

Leaning against it, she felt like she weighed a thousand pounds. She just rested there, thinking about their conversation, what he wanted from her, and how she and Pat had had nearly the same conversation about a year ago. Word for word, almost precisely the same.

Genuine Risks

Sister Bernadette, the school's career counselor, smiled warmly as Gennie entered the closet-like office for her belated and oft-put-off required pre-graduation consultation. Posters from colleges from around the country wallpapered the faded green walls, and brochures from the army, Peace Corps, and other local recruiters were stacked neatly in a plastic display on the edge of the desk. "Genuine Harrison, how do you do? I'm Sister Bernadette, and I've been looking over your school records, so I know you're a good student." She looked down at the open file stuffed with papers all about Gennie and tapped her pen on the top sheet. "Is it right that you only took the ACT once?"

Gennie looked away from the posters on the wall. "Yes, when I enrolled here last summer, they said I should take it right away."

"But no SAT?"

"No, ma'am."

The counselor smiled. "That's OK. Your ACT scores are good enough to get you into most local schools." She flipped through the papers in the file, looking for something. "But, is this correct: no college applications yet?"

"Umm, no. Sorry. I haven't gotten around to that yet."

The counselor did her best to repress her shock. With a forced smile, she went on. "Well, if you're looking at state schools, you should still be OK. So let's talk about majors. Tell me about your personal interests, like hobbies, or what your favorite class was here in your brief St. Joe's career."

Gennie closed her lips tight and continued her study of the posters while she thought about what she was expected to say. "Well, I guess I like horses," she suggested.

Sister Bernadette smiled broadly. "Oh, most young women do. I even did my share of riding back in the day. So, would you like to eventually find a career that pays enough to afford to own horses? Or perhaps become a large animal veterinarian?"

Gennie turned her tight lips into a grin. "I guess I haven't thought too much about it. I've worked with horses at Kensington Downs since I was a kid."

"Oh!" Sister Bernadette said, "That's great to have real-world experience! That's a valuable insight for career planning. As you know, St. Joe's likes to help our seniors find out what the future holds for them. But with only a few months left in the school year, you don't have much time, dear, especially if you are going to try for financial assistance. I suggest you hunker down and get some applications in this week. I see you live with your mother," Sister Bernadette noted sadly. "Are financial problems an area of concern?" She cocked her head and wrinkled her face in concern and sympathy.

"No, no, not at all. My mother's a restaurant manager, and she's already offered her help if I want to go to college."

"Oh, I see. *If* you go to college. A gap year, maybe? Or perhaps you've considered alternatives other than college? We have programs for the Peace Corps and other organizations where you can do valuable service while seeing the world and figuring out what you want to be doing and still leave plenty of time for college." She smiled.

"Well, no," Gennie mumbled, looking around the room for other ideas.

"Technical training? We have some wonderful summer internships. They're usually for juniors, but I can see if we can make an exception. If you took the business tech class, they should have informed you …"

Gennie shrugged. "Really, my main interest is in horses. I'd like to own and train them. I know some people in the field, so, I mean, I know it may not be common, but—"

Sister Bernadette looked stumped. "Well, horse ownership and training are very much a business, and I urge you to examine the benefits of a good business administration degree. Hobbies don't often earn you a living. You have to know how to manage money wisely to be profitable enough to provide enough income for living expenses, insurance, savings… Here are a few brochures for some local colleges with very good programs. Even the local technical college offers some programs that would benefit you long-term. They will take applications this late in the game. Please look them over and come see me again if you want help with your applications or anything. But, dear, you need to hurry. Nearly everyone else is already accepted into their colleges of choice."

"Yeah, I've rarely been like nearly everyone else," Gennie said, avoiding her eyes, then took the pamphlets and thanked her on her way out the door.

***

Anita had forgotten to bring her history book to school and asked Gennie if she could quickly grab her book out of her locker. Gennie gave her the locker combination and rushed down the hall to her next class. Anita ran to the locker and opened it. She grabbed the book and saw the row of pictures hidden along the inside wall of Gennie's locker. She recognized the group shot as some of the drunken boys at Gennie's apartment that night last fall. She saw a picture of an older jockey in his helmet and silks from a yellowed newspaper clipping and read the caption "Hank Harrison." She squinted at an eight-by-ten photo of a jockey aboard a horse in the winner's circle. She finally recognized him as the cute guy at the apartment that night. "Jockeys?" she said out loud, but the bell rang, and she had to slam the door and rush to her history class.

***

Gennie and Ray were doing homework at Gennie's apartment when Ray abruptly closed his book. "Have you decided what you're going to do? I mean, about college?" he asked. He sounded impatient. She always changed the subject whenever he brought it up.

"No, I guess I keep putting it off. I don't feel it's the only option, though. I don't feel pressure that it's now or never, you know? A gap year couldn't hurt."

"But a gap year for what? How can you keep putting it off? Graduation is just a few weeks away! What other option is there? I mean, if you don't go to college, what are you going to do?" He had put down his pen and looked at her intently.

She kept looking at her book. "I'll get a job. No big deal."

"Doing what? And why? Are you saving up to afford a fancy school? It really surprises me that you're not concerned about college."

She glanced up. "I guess school has always taken a backseat to the real world for me. What's the big deal?"

"The real world? Have you ever even had a 'real' job?"

She didn't like his condescending tone but knew that he knew nothing about what she did before starting school at St. Joe's. He worked fifteen hours a week at a hardware store, on top of keeping up good grades and being on the basketball team. She did nothing else beyond school besides the occasional intramural volleyball game and Greenpeace bake sale. To an outsider, it did look like she had it pretty easy. And that made her snap.

"Ray, would it shock and appall you to know that I'm turning nineteen this year and that I dropped out of high school for a year—yes, you're hanging out with a former dropout—and I survived mostly on my own 'in the real world'? So I guess I already took a gap year before it was cool. Why not do it again?" She was surprised to hear the anger in her voice and shocked to listen to herself admit she had dropped out. Her neck was hot; her face burning. Why did this rage come on so quickly? Why did the truth fall out so easily? Why was she at peace with the fact that he might get up and walk out the door now that he knew?

He remained calm, looking at her intently. "No, no, it wouldn't at all. That would explain a lot, actually. Thanks for finally telling me."

She again looked down at her book. Her heart was pounding so hard she thought she could see it through her sweater. She couldn't believe she had just said all that out loud.

"Aren't you going to tell me more? What did you do for a year? Was it because of your dad or something?"

"It's a year that I feel it's best to forget for a while so that I can get on and finish school with decent grades. That's really all I want to say about it."

"It must have been tough for you." Ray's voice sounded sincere.

"Actually, it wasn't tough at all, and I loved every minute of it. Maybe that's why I want to forget it." She finally looked up at him to emphasize her point.

"Oh, OK, that's cool if you don't want to talk about it," he shrugged. "I'll have to leave it to my imagination if you were an exotic dancer, or truck driver, or plumber for a year …"

She sighed, smiled, and let her pulse return to an average rate. "I'm sorry it probably won't live up to your colorful imagination. And after homecoming, you know exotic dancing is not a possibility. I just—I'm not ready, is all."

Ray studied her eyes and smiled. "That's fine. I don't understand, but OK. I guess I was just kinda wondering if we might think of school options together, that's all, but if you think it's a stupid idea, that's OK."

"What?" she asked, trying to tone down her anger.

"I just think it's weird that we've spent just about every moment we can together for eight months and that we've never discussed maybe going to college together. Maybe even away to the same school. Because I just enjoy studying with you. A lot."

She knew he had been accepted to all the schools he applied to and even had some invitations to play basketball at D3 schools. But he was going to wait to make his decision based on her? She sighed and threw a balled-up piece of paper at him. "I'm sorry. I guess I just never thought about that."

"You really didn't, huh?" He sounded melancholy. She didn't answer. They both looked down at the table.

***

The following Saturday, Anita came to Gennie's apartment to do homework. As usual, the TV was on in the background. The afternoon sports show announced a Kentucky Derby prep race that would be broadcast in an hour. Gennie's head shot up, and she intently watched the day's field summary. Anita kept writing. "Know any of those people?" she asked.

"Huh?" Gennie responded, turning to look at her in surprise.

"I guessed your family is into horse racing. I saw the pictures in your locker. Are any of them in that race?"

Gennie sighed. She was caught. "No, no. That's the real big time."

"Your dad was a jockey, huh?"

Gennie sighed deeply. "Yep. He died in a spill."

"Oh my God!" Anita gasped. "Tell me you're kidding."

"Wish I were."

"Is your cousin a jockey?"

"No, he wanted to be one, but he got too tall. He's the starter at Kensington Downs—he's the guy who pushes the button to open the gate at the start of the race."

"But Pat's a jockey," Anita said. "I saw the picture."

Gennie smiled. "Yeah, he's a very good rider. He could actually go places."

"That's got to be exciting."

"It is." Gennie gave a little laugh. "I'm even named for a horse, Genuine Risk. She was one of the few fillies—a female horse—to win the Kentucky Derby." She suddenly wanted to tell Anita everything. It felt so good to have the secret released. She wanted to tell Anita about Pat, the real story about Pat, and about her mother, and about living in the backstretch, and maybe give her an introductory lesson on horse racing, but she stopped there and turned back to her paper. She knew she couldn't let the story get out beyond her apartment, and she knew Anita couldn't keep a good story quiet, even if she tried.

"So the Derby is on May 1? Same day as College Decision Day," Anita noted as the commercial ended.

"Hmm," Gennie said while staring at the screen, even though it had moved on to another commercial. "Isn't that ironic?"

"Do you still go to the races? Could you take me sometime?" Anita asked, seeming to be genuinely interested. "I could write a story about it! Our school is so close to the track. I'm surprised I haven't thought of that myself!"

Gennie looked down at her work. "No, I haven't been back at all, not since my dad died. My home is here now."

Anita squinted in confusion. "What? You've never been back to go watch the races? To see your cousin?"

Gennie shook her head slowly. "Impossible," she said, so quietly she could barely hear herself.

And so the dam Gennie built was starting to experience some leaks. Her story was getting out there. It seemed the two people closest to her were more intrigued than repelled by her background than she expected. Was she ready to let them know everything? Or had she made a mistake by letting her guard down? Did it matter with just one month left of school? For the first time, Gennie wasn't thinking about what others thought of her. She was thinking of what she thought of them and how much they meant to her. Even though she hadn't realized it yet, we know that she was worried about letting her new friends down. Imagine that. Like that dam, our stoic heroine's stone facade was sprouting some leaks.

Getting the Rebound

Gennie sat alone behind the high school on a bench overlooking the track field. Spring was in full bloom, with the grass turning bright green and buds sprouting on the trees seemingly overnight. A strong wind brought with it warmth she hadn't felt in months. Each day held more light than darkness.

She had a pile of college pamphlets in her lap that Ray had given her to look over. He had been offered scholarships to so many colleges that she had no idea how he would decide. Gennie had read all of the brochures and was envious of what they had to offer. One of them even had equine studies and a business program. She was sure Ray would have a great time and excel at any of the schools in any program. She was also sure none of them were for her. Sylvia had again made an offer to pay for college to get Gennie to commit to any of them. But Gennie told her that if she went to college, she would prefer to pay for it herself.

She looked at her watch and saw she had twenty minutes to get to O'Casey's. Even though it was only a five-minute walk, she got up quickly, dropping some pamphlets and running after them as they tumbled away in the wind. She tried to walk slowly so she wouldn't be too early, but she wanted to be the first one there so she could grab a back booth. Her heart was racing, and she knew it wasn't from getting up too fast.

As soon as she entered, she saw Pat. He had chosen to sit in the front section so she wouldn't miss him. He must have been there a while because he already had a Diet Coke. "You're early," she said with a smile as she slid into the booth, forgetting to scan the restaurant for familiar faces.

"So are you," he answered coyly. Gennie thought he looked exceptionally handsome, even though he was just in jeans and a pullover. She could tell he had just gotten a haircut.

"How are you?" she asked, really meaning it.

He shrugged. "My numbers are good this season. Rob's kept me busy."

"I saw you won the Chance Stakes last weekend. That's great."

"Yeah, but I won the track ping-pong tournament last week, too. Beat out Ruben for the first time—really ticked him off."

Gennie laughed. "Winning the ping-pong tournament is a bigger deal to you than winning a graded stakes race?"

His face turned stern and serious as he stared at her. "Did you hear me? I finally beat Ruben. This is big."

She shook her head in disbelief and sighed. "I could still whip you."

"I'd like to see you try," he said, looking her in the eyes until she looked away.

The waitress came, greeted Gennie by name, and asked if she wanted to order something. Even though her stomach was in knots, she ordered a milkshake. Pat smiled at her. "Wow, the waitresses know you at O'Casey's now. How appropriate."

Gennie remembered all the times they mocked the kids in there. She had no right to contradict him. "I know, I know. I just wanted to blend in, you know. It was just part of the package."

He nodded. "OK, sure, I get that. So what else comes with this 'package' deal?"

"Well," she began and caught the eye of one of the girls sitting across the room. It was Susan, Ray's neighbor, and Gennie cringed. She knew Ray was working at the hardware store that afternoon, and she had hoped his friends wouldn't be around either. She regained her composure and began again, "Well, it's the end of the school year. I'm almost done. Just four more weeks, and I'm out of here." She laughed nervously. "And I guess I called you because I wanted some advice."

"That's easy," he said, looking into his glass of fizzing cola. "Come back to the track and work with Rob for a while until you can co-own a horse or two like we talked about a year ago."

She grinned, biting her lower lip. "Um, I didn't even tell you what advice I was looking for."

"Oh, OK," he nodded. "I'm sorry. You know me—Mr. Just Jump Right In."

"But since you brought it up, do you think that is an option? Is Rob hiring help?"

Pat let out a quiet laugh and shook his head. "You know for a fact that Rob would hire you. Hell, he'd adopt you if you asked him. He must mention you and Hank ten times a day, every day. I have to tell him to shut up."

"Really? I assumed everybody would've forgotten about me by now."

Pat just made a "humph" noise. They were both quiet for a moment. The waitress thankfully brought Gennie's shake to break the silence.

Gennie fumbled at trying to get the paper off her straw. Her hands were trembling. "I'm sorry I didn't call … or visit. I didn't know if I should or not."

"I guess I didn't expect you to."

"But you didn't call either," she said, stabbing at her shake with the finally unwrapped straw.

"I didn't think you wanted me to," he replied quietly. "You made it pretty clear you needed your space."

She watched her shake become a blur as her eyes welled with tears. She took a deep breath, trying to hold them back. "So, have you thought about me, or us, since I've been gone?"

"Ever think of you?" Pat sat back and looked at her incredulously for a moment. Then he leaned forward so he didn't have to speak loudly. "You're all I ever think about. If I'm not on a horse going forty miles per hour, believe me, I'm thinking about you. At the diner. Watching TV. Playing ping-pong. Even, goddamn it, brushing my teeth. I started thinking maybe I need professional help because it's been so bad."

Gennie looked down, her head swimming with his words.

He continued. "I thought of all the things I did wrong. I should've taken you out more. Treated you more like a girlfriend instead of just—I dunno. I should've spoiled you. I guess our whole … whatever … 'relationship' just always seemed so natural, I took it for granted. I should have never taken it for granted. I should've known there was a chance you'd leave for something better. Of course, you would. Why stay stuck at a low-grade track with a bunch of dirty losers …"

"Stop it," she snapped, finally looking up. "Pat, just stop. I'm sorry you've been torturing yourself, but all that—it's crap. Don't ever think that again. Everything about us was perfect. Maybe not traditional or how other people do it, but there's nothing about us that's traditional anyway. I never wanted anything more. I couldn't possibly have wanted more from you, from us."

He rubbed his hand over his hair, then stared at her, looking exhausted and confused.

"Then why would you leave like that? Just leave. One day you're there every minute, and then next, poof! Gone. Totally gone, never to be heard from again … well, except when you thought I was dying in the hospital—and now."

"To finish high school, Pat. Just to finish high school. You may recall that I watched my dad die on that track. In less than five seconds, the sport I loved more than anything became the one I hated with every ounce of my being." She quickly wiped away the tears that had now started to escape down her cheek. "So maybe when Sylvia gave me the option of not having to stare every day at that damn dirt where I'll always see him sprawled like that—" She stopped to take a deep breath. "Yeah, Pat, I wanted to get away. I had to get away. But not from you. Just from every single thing you're associated with."

Pat stared into his glass and sighed. "I don't know how to help you with that, Gennie. I've seen my share of disaster on the track, too. You know spills happen sometimes. But you know these people are racing because they love it. It's all they want to do. If they get hurt, even if they die, they were doing something they loved, that was in their blood." She still looked down but nodded. "It's OK to be pissed about what happened, but accidents happen everywhere, Gennie, in every job, on every street, and even in every house. And those people didn't die doing what they loved. That's got to be worth something. You can't blame your old home for what happened. I know it's hard, but I know you can find a way to remember more of the good times than the bad. I can try and help you." He looked for her eyes, but she remained staring at the table. "I want to try to help you."

When she remained silent, staring at the table, he reached for some of the pamphlets she had set beside her. His face turned even more sullen as he saw what they were.

"So now are you trying to run even further away to college?" he asked, flipping through them.

Her eyes followed his hands on the brochures. "That was the advice I was looking for. Sylvia's offering to pay for college, and I don't know if I should take her up on it or if I even want to go. Everyone else in school is already admitted to where they want to go and think I'm a loser freak."

"Sylvia's turned into the picture-perfect mother now, hasn't she?" he said with an edge.

"Pat, she's been OK, really. You can't blame her for trying. But what do you think of college? What would you do?"

"What would I do? Become a rider instead, like I did, but I can't blame someone for wanting to go to college. I just don't know how much good it does a person who doesn't really want to be there. I mean, I don't have any regrets about not going. What would you study?"

She shrugged. "Maybe business because if I own horses one day, it might be beneficial."

He nodded. "Yeah, maybe, but the most successful horse people I know don't even have high school diplomas."

"Yeah, I know," she agreed. She continued to stir the shake. "Do you have a—a personal opinion about my decision?" she asked, too afraid to look up at him.

"Yes, sure, I do." He answered more quickly than she expected.

When he didn't continue, she finally looked at him to see that was exactly what he was waiting for.

Once she had her eyes on him, he spoke, "My personal opinion is that if you do go to college, I would just ask that you go somewhere with a track so I could move there, too."

She looked away in surprise, her eyes were wide, and she couldn't resist a big tight smile that she tried to hide. Pat smiled, too, happy to have shocked her. "You could never leave Rob. He needs you," she said.

"I don't care about what he needs."

She sighed and tried to hold back another smile. "Well, OK, then. Thanks for making that decision a lot easier." She sucked another mouthful of the shake.

"I told you once I'd always be available for advice," he said softly.

"That's why I called."

"I'm really glad you did."

"I'm not sure I am." They both smiled and got up. Pat insisted on taking the bill to the checkout counter, but Gennie left a tip on the table. He held the door for her as they went. Gennie was still aware of the curious eyes watching her leave the diner with someone who wasn't Ray.

Pat offered to drive her home, and she accepted. She noticed that she didn't need to remind him of the address. As they pulled up to her building, she started to thank him for the ride and meeting her, but he cut her off as he reached around her shoulder and pulled her toward him into a long, warm kiss. She had forgotten how nice he felt, how natural, how comfortable.

He released her, but she didn't back away.

"I miss you," he said, lifting her chin to look her in the eyes.

She couldn't answer, couldn't breathe, couldn't think. She shut her eyes and was silent for a long time. "Me, too," she said and slowly got out of the car. She felt herself hoping Pat would call her name. But he didn't. He didn't have to.

Benched

Anita was nervous about the clandestine meeting Ray had set up. "What could he possibly want from me?" she wondered. He had texted her the night before to say he wanted to talk to her privately about something. She was to meet him in the library after her last class. Her mind raced with the possibilities … maybe he was really in love with her and needed to know if she felt the same way before he broke up with Gennie. Or maybe one of his friends wanted to go out with her. Or maybe he wanted help with buying Gennie a ring. She wouldn't be surprised. She could feel her heart pounding as she approached the library. She looked down the hall to make sure no one saw her enter. She had even worn darker clothes than her usual bright colors and patterns. She didn't want to be noticed.

Ray was waiting at a table along the windows. He had homework in front of him but saw her as soon as she walked in.

"Thanks for coming," he said. "I really appreciate it. I hope you can help me out."

Anita sat down slowly, trying to be quiet. "What's up?" she asked cautiously, trying to sound nonchalant.

He sighed. "Well, you know Gennie better than anyone else." She shrugged. "And I was just wondering if you had a better idea than me of what her long-term plans are. I mean, just when I think we're like good friends—tight, you know?—she gets really cold and private and secretive, and then I feel like I don't know her at all."

"Hello?" she said mockingly. "Join the club! You know she's like that. That's probably what attracted you to her in the first place—you and tons of other guys, I hear." As soon as she said that, she regretted it. She bit her lip in embarrassment and looked down at the desktop.

"I know. Go on," Ray encouraged.

Anita sighed. She'd gone this far, and, if she was being honest with herself, it was nice to talk about some of this. Her journal was only good for so much. "I think her 'mystique' is what makes her so interesting to people. I honestly don't know if she does it purposely to get attention and to drive us nuts, or sometimes, yeah, I wonder if she's one of these TV or movie types with a secret second life somewhere. Maybe she's a pop star by night, or a special agent, or an exotic dancer. I don't know any more than you."

Ray made a tight-lipped smile. "Well, at least that makes me feel a little better that it's not just me. Have you guys talked about college?"

"She knows where I'm going, and I told her to come with me to Chicago, too, but she just blows me off."

Ray looked out the window. "I feel really, really childish about this, but has she ever talked to you about us?"

"As if!" she exclaimed and then quickly looked around to see if she had disturbed anyone. "Are you kidding? I beg for details and she ignores me like I'm invisible or something." When she stopped talking, she realized she probably shouldn't have said that either. She bit her lower lip again as she felt her face burning.

Ray smiled. "She told me she left school for a year to work before coming here."

"What?" Anita yelped as quietly as she could.

"C'mon, you must have known that. You can't tell her I told you; I assumed you knew. Did she ever mention any type of job to you?"

Anita sat back in her chair, soaking in this revelation about her friend, and then started to put together connections. "Well, I know her family was into horse racing and her dad was a jockey, but that's all I know. And you can't tell her I told you that, so now we're even."

He nodded, absorbing the new piece of evidence. "OK, one more question, and I'll stop prying. Susan, next door to me, asked me if we broke up because she saw Gennie with some guy she didn't recognize at O'Casey's. You don't have to tell me if you don't want to, but I was wondering if you knew who he was. I'm hoping it was a brother or something."

Anita scrunched her forehead in concentration. "No, she doesn't have a brother," she said seriously, not catching Ray's wishful attempt at humor. "What did he look like?"

"I don't know," Ray answered, "other than he had dark hair and was shorter than me, Susan said."

With that, Anita raised her eyebrows in consideration but answered, "Well, she does have a cousin I met once, but other than that, I have no idea who it could have been, but I wish I did."

Ray sighed and looked back out the window.

***

Gennie found herself trying not to be at home as the school year wound down. She often stayed at school, working in the computer lab or doing homework in the cafeteria. She often went to her mother's restaurant to have dinner and do homework in a back booth. She would keep her phone in "do not disturb" mode. But one night, as she got home, she found Ray sitting on a couch in the apartment building's lobby.

"Oh, hi," she said, surprised. "Did I forget something we were supposed to do?"

"Uh, yeah, like talk to each other?" he suggested.

"Oh, Ray," she said with a nervous laugh as she opened the door for them to go to the elevator, "Yeah, I'm sorry I haven't been around much. I've been helping Mom out at the restaurant this week, and my homework has just piled up with all those stupid final papers …"

"And going to O'Casey's with other guys … I know it must be a hectic schedule." The elevator doors closed them in with perfect timing.

She looked up at him with a look of remorse and surprise. "Susan, huh?" she asked.

He nodded.

"Oh, I figured that snoop would go and spread some kind of childish rumor as soon as I saw her there, staring at me," she said lightheartedly.

"Hmm, it doesn't sound like much of a rumor if it's true," he suggested, holding her backpack as she opened the apartment door.

"Well, yes, I was there with someone who, Heaven forbid, I didn't get your—or Susan's—permission to go with, and if I felt it was important to you, I think I would have told you myself," she said, proud of her smugness.

"Well, that leads me to believe that is why you suddenly haven't talked to me for the past week." She took her backpack, and he went to sit on her couch. "I probably shouldn't have just showed up here, but I figured it was my right since I'm normally here every Thursday night anyway. It's TV night, and a ritual is a ritual," he added, trying to lighten the mood.

She stood against the kitchen counter, her arms folded together. She was quiet for a long time as he used the remote to flip channels until he finally looked up at her to see what she was doing. Their eyes met, and she was the first to look away. She walked over and sat next to him. She took the remote from his hands and turned the TV off.

"I was just thinking," she said, "that you're probably right. I think I have been avoiding you this week because I'm feeling kind of overwhelmed right now with the end of school and all these decisions and stuff. And I think with you around, it makes some of my decisions harder."

He sat back. "And Mystery Man makes decisions easier?"

She smiled and shook her head. "Mystery Man is just an old friend with a good shoulder to lean on."

"'Old friend.' That's problem number one. We know what that phrase means. And, if I'm correct in my assumption, it probably means I wouldn't want you leaning on any part of him."

"Well, I'm sorry, Ray, that's not something you can have a say about."

He looked her in the eyes. "I have two shoulders which are bigger than his, I hear."

She smiled sadly and looked away. "They are fine shoulders, I'll admit. But maybe I shouldn't be leaning on anyone right now. I think we both need to make independent decisions, and if they happen to cross, that means something, and if they don't cross, that means something, too."

"Well, OK," he sighed, getting up. "Last time I invite myself to my own breakup. But I guess I'm glad I did, so I can stop wasting my time calling you every night. It will give me more time to study for finals and brush up on watching TV alone and going out with the guys again. They've all been on my case lately. Oh, and I suppose the prom is out, huh? That's OK; that'll save a ton of money actually." He was talking fast, without breathing. He caught himself, stopped, and sighed with a tight-lipped smile. He looked at her once, hoping she would tell him his assumptions were all wrong and then left the apartment when he saw she kept her eyes down and had no intention of speaking.

Gennie stared at the closed door for a long time as her heart went from pounding madly back to its usual pace. Then she stared at the dark TV screen as she felt tears stream down her cheeks, then onto her neck. She reached for her phone, but her hands were shaking too much to use it. It was probably for the best, she thought and threw the phone back down.

And so our heroine took charge of her narrative, or at least something inside her did. Time was moving along and taking her with it, as it often does with all of us. But who did she almost call? Unfortunately, she wouldn't tell.

The Final Turn

Ah, the last month of the school year. Whether you were looking forward to graduation or just summer vacation, you were excited. But for seniors, May was all about them. While the rest of the classes were slammed preparing for finals, the seniors weren't panicked. Most knew those final grades weren't going to affect them since they were already admitted to college. They were so done with high school, except, of course, for the fun end-of-year stuff: Prom. Final concerts. Final art shows. Final assemblies. Senior Skip Day. And, of course, College Admission Day. Colorful pennants from all the various schools the seniors were admitted to were hung throughout the Commons, and photos were taken of friends by friends. And so much hugging. The small class of seniors seemed to, for the most part, become pretty close during their years—or year—together.

For Gennie, she kept herself busy that last month of school: finishing up projects, studying for finals (unlike most seniors), and planning for the summer and life beyond high school. She tried to stay focused on her schoolwork but found herself checking her phone often for messages that never came. Despite the nearly constant overwhelming urge to call Ray to talk about classes, and finals, and his plans, she didn't. Despite trying to tell herself she was above teenage drama, she couldn't help but notice as he purposely avoided her by changing to the other side of the hall when walking by and talking loudly with his other friends so that it would appear he wasn't even aware of her presence. She knew he wasn't a loud talker. Now even he seemed to be auditioning for the drama club. And with their lockers in the same hallway, it was inevitable that she would have to watch Susan's suddenly frequent appearances at his locker and observe how they seemed to walk into every class together. Gennie tried to look away, both physically and mentally, but she couldn't. Luckily, Ray had more willpower than she did and never turned back to see if she was watching him. Anita, of course, was quick to fill her in on the gossip about the pair's new relationship: how Ray was voted prom king but walked out of the gym instead of going up on stage to accept the crown and how Susan was planning the end-of-school party to end all parties at a swanky downtown club. Anita doubted that either one of them would be invited.

"I'm happy for them," Gennie said as they ate their lunch alone at their standard cafeteria table.

"You are lying through your teeth, and I know it," Anita answered between kale salad bites.

"No, really, I think she's good for his ego right now, which is what he needs," Gennie said. "I mean, it won't last. He's definitely on the rebound from me, don't get me wrong." She smiled uncharacteristically.

Anita shrugged. "I just wish you could have put a plug in for me before you dumped him like that."

"I did not 'dump' him," she argued. "Who's saying that?"

"The whole world knows. He's practically bragging about it," Anita said. "You know, it's cool to be sensitive these days. I'm sure that's how Susan got in. 'Let me comfort you, Ray after that big meanie new girl was so cruel and heartless to you …'."

Ray and Susan walked by as if on cue, and Gennie tried to smile at him, but he never looked her way, and Susan was too busy talking to him that she didn't notice Gennie, either. After they passed, she whispered to Anita, "Oh, yeah, he's hurting real bad." She thought she said it jokingly, but she found herself thinking that Susan could afford nice clothes, and it looked like she had her eyebrows professionally done … and then Gennie quickly tried to think about something else instead.

***

Ray finished his last exam and closed the booklet. He looked around the room at the rest of the kids still writing, including Gennie in the corner. It looked like she was also finishing up. He carried his papers to the teacher, who shook his hand and wished him well at college. "Keep in touch—can't wait to hear about your games," the teacher told him. Ray thanked him and walked out into the hallway. He put his backpack on a table full of summer club handouts and pretended to be putting something away in it.

Gennie came walking out a few minutes later and almost walked into him. "Oh, I'm sorry," she said. "I guess I was in a hurry to get out of there."

"Was that your last one, too?" he asked, zipping up the near-empty bag.

"Yeah," she smiled, "it's all over."

"Yeah, me, too," he said. "Off to the big time now."

"Me too," she said.

They began walking down the hall together. "What have you decided is going to be your big time?" he asked casually.

"Working," she answered securely. "I figure that if after a year I feel I'm missing something by not being in college, I'll go then. I won't be too much of an old lady in another year."

"Are you going to keep living with Sylvia?"

"Well, no. She announced that she's moving to St. Louis to open another restaurant for her dad. She begged me to go with her and to go to school there, but … I don't think so. I'll be staying with a family friend for a while. What about you? What are you doing this summer?" She looked into his eyes but then quickly looked away.

"I'll be full time at the hardware store. I need the money. So I don't know, no wild plans for the last summer of my youth. My folks aren't speaking at all anymore, so that'll be a pain in the ass. My mom bawls every time I go visit Dad, so who knows how that's going to work out."

"That's tough. I'm sorry."

He shrugged. "I'm actually glad to be going away to have some space. Probably selfish of me, but whatever." Now he made the mistake of looking into her eyes. "So maybe we could keep in touch over the summer, I mean, since we'll both be working and probably bored as adults."

Gennie froze. "Well, my job, it's more than full time. It's kind of like all the time. Calling me will be tough. I mean, it's weird hours …"

The spell was broken. Ray shook his head and put up his hands. "I'm not trying to stalk you. I just thought maybe we could keep in touch as friends. Friends only, fine, OK, no big deal. Whatever. I tried. Well, I've got to go. See you at graduation." He turned down the hallway and disappeared before Gennie had a chance to recover from her rudeness.

She sighed deeply, knowing she blew a chance to mend fences, but then realized she had done the right thing. There was no way she could let her two lives mingle together so casually. It was all or nothing. It was always all or nothing.

***

Carl got the news from Rob and had to stand back to lean against the wall. "She's coming back?" he asked in disbelief.

"Starting next week. Gosh, I got to say I don't know if it's the right thing for her to do, though. She really should go to college. She could do something with herself, you know? She's got that Hank gusto that could be useful if used in the right way, you know what I'm saying?"

"Yeah, yeah, I do," Carl agreed. "She's a smart girl. And she's smart enough to make her own decisions. She went back and got her high school diploma. That was smart, especially making Sylvia pick up the tab for a fancy school. That was really smart."

"She said graduation is Saturday morning."

"Saturday?"

"Saturday."

"Before post time?"

"Before post time."

"I'd kinda like to see that," Carl said.

"Me too," Rob agreed.

"Should we crash it?" Carl asked, eyebrows raised.

Rob grinned and nodded. "Yes, yes, I think we should. I bet a few others would come along, too. But I'm not really a betting man ..." Both men laughed and went about their morning routines.

***

The auditorium was buzzing with excitement. Families assembled to watch their children receive their diplomas and awards. The seniors adjusted their hats and gowns and wondered who invented such stupid outfits. Girls borrowed each other's bobby pins and hairspray in the locker room. The guys made fun of each other for wearing dresses and played Frisbee across the benches with their mortarboards. The teachers supervised and tried to keep the mood serious but couldn't help but envy the energy and excitement of the students. Mothers in the auditorium discreetly dabbed tears from their eyes while reading the program and thinking about how quickly life flies by. As the time to line up got nearer, some of their daughters also got teary eyed and sentimental, testing their waterproof mascara and hugging kids they barely knew, promising to keep in touch.

The Junior Orchestra began playing, and the hall was hushed as the line of students in black caps and gowns proceeded through the aisles, smiling and sneaking secret waves to their families as they passed by. The class had 120 graduates, and they all filed into their seats in the front of the auditorium. The various speakers talked about the hope for the future and the endless possibilities for each student. They spoke of no one definition of success, no one gauge of happiness. They spoke of higher education, marriage, jobs, and adventures that awaited all of them. The valedictorian thanked the teachers, the coaches, and the parents; the principal thanked the senior class for setting a good example; and a priest blessed the graduating class and wished them well. Then the names were read, and the students walked across the stage one by one to accept their magical, symbolic piece of paper and to smile for the flashing cameras.

Despite the warning from the principal to, "Hold all applause until the very end," each student received warm congratulations from the crowd with customized cheers from their friends and family. Gennie was dreading the awkwardness of being the only one to get just a smattering of applause since her mom and her mom's date were the only people she had invited. She was pretty sure Ray and his friends wouldn't clap. Anita would, but she was right behind her in line and couldn't do much when she was already on stage. So Gennie was shocked to the point of turning away from the principal when her name was announced, and a roar of whoops and hollers shook the hall from the back. Ray and Anita also turned from their positions to see who the fan club was. Gennie tried to hide her grin as she saw the group of trackers way in the back, giving her the loudest and most raucous standing ovation of the event. A city newspaper photographer captured her shy smile and published it with a caption of how it was graduation day across the city for senior classes. Her first picture in the newspaper would be cut out and saved, along with the countless copies of those of her father and Pat.

When the ceremony was finished, and people moved out onto the high school's front lawn for photos and more congratulations, Gennie found herself sprinting to her old track friends and ignoring that she should probably go to her mother first. Rob gave her a warm congratulatory hug, Carl, Ruben, Harry, and John gave her high fives, and Pat lifted her off her feet in a swirling hug and kiss. As she was let down, she smiled at him and said, "Do you realize the scandal that this may have just caused?" as she saw Anita whispering to Ray behind them.

"Do you care?" he asked sincerely. She thought about it and let her eyes wander to see if Anita and Ray were looking at her.

"I guess I don't need to anymore," she answered, watching her two school friends walk away.

"Here, for you, just a little something," Pat said, handing her a perfectly wrapped small square box with a big gold bow.

She stared at it, startled and speechless.

Suddenly, behind her, she heard her mother's familiar sarcastic voice say, "Gennie, do I get to say congratulations?" Gennie spun around in embarrassment.

"Mom! I'm sorry! Thank you!" she said, giving her a one-armed hug while she protected the small gift box. She smiled weakly at Sylvia's new boyfriend, who seemed equally uncomfortable. Sylvia looked at the group of trackers and diplomatically said hello to Rob, Carl, and Pat, the only ones she knew. Gennie eyed them as if to warn them to be nice to her, and they all politely congratulated her on Gennie's success.

Then Gennie sought out Anita to congratulate her and to thank her for all her help over the past school year. "You taught me everything I really needed to know," she told her with a hug. Anita smiled and told her to keep in touch over the summer so they could do some stuff and go to more movies before she left for school. Gennie said she'd call her and then went back to her group, where only Sylvia and the boyfriend remained.

"Post time's approaching," Sylvia explained dryly as she saw Gennie looking around for her track friends. Gennie nodded, understanding their sudden disappearance, and the three began to leave for lunch at one of the town's nicest restaurants. Gennie heard someone running up from behind her as they walked to the car. It was Ray.

"Hey, congratulations!" he said, hugging her.

"You too," she said, returning the hug and meaning it. She saw his parents several yards away, standing silent and stone-faced. "It looks like they're thrilled to be doing the parental duties together," she said quietly.

"This could rate as one of the worst days of my life," he said quietly with a smile, so no one would hear or guess what he had said.

"I'm sorry," she said. "You could come to lunch with my mom and her new love interest and talk about politically acceptable things in front of a teenage daughter," she offered.

"Hmm, the option is tempting, but I don't need my mom sobbing all over me again today."

They looked at each other in awkward silence. Gennie sighed and started. "Ray, I'm sorry I was such a ... disappointment these past few weeks. You deserve better than that."

"Thank you for saying that. I'll admit I wish the year would have ended differently."

"You know you'll do great in college and everything. You don't need me."

"You'd make it easier." His eyes were intense. The gleeful mood of the morning was instantly gone.

"Ray, don't. I can't do it. I can't—"

"I know, I know you can't. I won't say I understand, but maybe you'll—I don't know." Ray hugged her again and whispered in her ear, "I love you," and then he walked back to his parents. Gennie noticed that Susan was there now talking with them, and all three were smiling. She genuinely felt sorry for Ray. She watched for a second more and then walked back to the car waiting for her.

"He's such a nice boy, Gennie, really," Sylvia said as they moved through the parking lot. "He seems bright like he'll go somewhere. I know you don't care about my opinion, but I still wish you'd consider going to college with him. Just try that first, and if it doesn't work out, then go back to the track."

Gennie just shrugged and got into the backseat, where she set the box from Pat on her lap. She told herself that it was too big to be a ring box but then thought those fancy jewelry store boxes could be pretty big. If it wasn't jewelry, what else could it be? A watch. That's it—a watch. A traditional graduation gift. She slowly pulled off the bow and tugged the ribbon off the box. Carefully, so she didn't make too much noise and distract Sylvia from her conversation with the boyfriend, she removed the paper. Underneath was a plain black box with a lid. She tugged it off and looked inside. She reached in and pulled out a perfectly pristine, never-been-used, shiny white ping-pong ball. She laughed, then smiled and looked out the window, watching the blur of hugs, tears, and smiles fade into the distance.

And so our heroine drove away from a blip in her heart monitor, a bridge of her song, a sidetrack of life's journey. She left behind her a screen-worthy setting of average teenagers basking in the sun of American normalcy. But once you've been part of that scene, can you ever really leave it behind? Or does it become part of you? Does it stay inside, lingering and festering, until you return to it? Does drinking the sweet elixir of normalcy poison you or cure you?

Post Time

Gennie woke up in a new bedroom for the third time in just one year. Unlike most American teens on an early summer morning, she sprung to attention right when the alarm went off, even though the sun was barely awake itself. She could see the outline of frilly lace curtains as the sun started its early summer morning ascent.

So it turns out that Gennie had called Rob, as he had told her she could do anytime, and taken him up on his offer to stay in his and his wife's stable-side bunk house on their small farm just outside the city. He offered her a grooming job with room and board until she had enough money to get a real apartment. She appreciated the privacy of having a separate apartment away from their house and loved walking out of her room and right into a stable. The apartment was a little too frilly for her taste—too many ruffles and pillows and multiple gingham patterns packed into a studio-sized space—but she wouldn't complain since the rent was free. The only personal decorations she added were the old lucky horseshoe and her bulletin board.

Mrs. Wayne was thrilled to have someone else around the property. Their only child, a son, had moved out five years previously to take a job in Kentucky. She had never enjoyed having an empty nest and seemed more than happy to care for "practically an orphan", as she described Gennie to the ladies at the salon.

Rob kept a few retired racehorses that his wife tended to. They seemed interested in the stranger who would walk by several times a day, cooing to them and handing them carrots. On Gennie's first morning on the job, the horses seemed disappointed to discover they weren't the reason she was rising early. She just walked past, rubbing their snouts and enjoying how comfortable her old riding boots were to walk around in again. Looking down at her legs, she remembered her uniform skirt and stark white legs and laughed.

Rob was already waiting for her in the car with two travel mugs filled with black coffee. "Mornin'," she said with a smile.

"Are you prepared for this?" Rob asked, more seriously than she expected.

"You bet," she answered, taking a sip. "I've been waiting for a long time."

"OK …" he said sarcastically and started the car. "And I'm not going to be a nag about this, cuz Lord knows that's what I have a wife for, but you know you still have time to register for classes at UC. It just seems to me that since you've got some steam behind you now with a diploma from that good high school …"

"Thanks, Rob, but I'm good. I know what I'm doing."

He stared at her a moment more, probably wondering what he should say or if it was any of his business to say anything more, then nodded silently and turned away to begin the drive in.

As they neared the track, Gennie stared out the window and took deep breaths.

Rob turned to look at her for the first time since they left the farm. "You sure you're OK? You sound like you're hyperventilating."

"No. Yes. I mean, sure, I'm fine. Maybe a little nervous. It's just weird being back. Is everyone going to remember me?"

"Is that it, or are you second-guessing your decision?"

Gennie stopped scanning the track's backstretch as he drove toward his designated spot in the employee lot, that area where she had directed Pat to all those years ago on the dark summer morning. She stared out the front window until Rob turned back to check on her. "No, no second-guessing. This is where I belong," she said quietly. "Definitely where I belong. It's just weird. A week ago, at this time, I would still be sleeping. Mom would be making breakfast. I'd be surrounded all day by kids whose biggest worries were what to wear to prom."

"Welcome to growing up," said Rob. "It happens to everyone, but to some, it happens earlier than others."

She nodded and went back to surveying the old familiar scene as Rob parked the car. It was a picture-perfect summer day with glistening dewy lawns and a peek of the sun causing an orange hue above the tops of the stables. She was glad everything was as she remembered it, especially the familiar scents of horse, leather, and old stable wood. They walked to Rob's stables, where Carl was waiting with a big smile. "Hey, Gennie, girl!" he said, rushing over with a warm hug. "It's good to have you home."

"It's nice to be here," she said, squeezing him tight. Her heart was pounding even faster, and she felt her eyes moisten. She quickly wiped her eyes, looking away as she did.

"Enough of the mush," Rob said jokingly. "Gennie, you'll work those four horses on the end. Only Medical Miracle is going to run this week, and we should get him on the track in a half hour before Jerry gets out there with his watch."

Gennie nodded in understanding and smiled at Carl, who nodded with a grin and left to prepare for the day. She started walking toward stall 12 at the dark end of the barn when Pat leaped from stall 11 with a large bouquet. "Welcome back," he said, smiling from ear to ear. She jumped and gasped, caught her breath, then bent down to rest both hands on her knees to process the shock. She was glad it was still dark in there so that he couldn't see her blushing and shaking with surprise.

She took a few deep breaths, straightened up, smiled, took the daisies, and punched him in the arm. He smiled and didn't flinch with the punch. Then he pulled her into as big of a hug as the flowers would allow. She pulled away and buried her nose into the bouquet. The only other time someone had given her flowers was Ray for homecoming. Pat squeezed her other hand tightly and said, "I'll let you get to work, but I'll meet you at the diner later, OK?"

She merely nodded with a shy smile.

She kept nodding and watched him dart away to his morning workout appointments. She put the flowers in a water bucket, wiped her eyes one more time, took a deep breath, and started grooming the tall gelding that had watched the entire proceedings with interest.

***

Gennie groomed the horses, mucked out their stalls, and then worked on cleaning up the stable area itself until lunchtime. She kept a smile the whole morning despite feeling the immediate effects of physical labor that she hadn't done for ten months.

The other grooms welcomed her back, and Milo informed her about a radio station that had changed formats. Rob took her to the track kitchen where, without hesitation, she ordered her favorite tuna melt with tomato even though it was only nine in the morning. A dozen people, from the guys behind the counter to nearly everyone at the tables, came up to Gennie to welcome her back. At one point, Rob snapped that people should leave her alone so she could eat, which made her smile more. Through a mouthful of tuna melt, she said, "My face actually hurts from smiling so much."

Rob wrinkled his eyebrows. "Are you sure it's not from eating so much? Geez, didn't your ma feed you these past few months?"

"You know, Sylvia is a really good cook, I'll give her that, but I did miss this kitchen." She laughed but didn't stop gobbling the french fries and carrot sticks. She saw Pat come in and waved him over. He sat down and took one of her fries.

"I wouldn't do that if I were you," Rob warned. "I've seen wolves less intent on their meals than this one here."

"Go get your own," she played along with a low growl, moving her plate closer to her.

Pat didn't play along. "I'm not too hungry before the races anyway."

She sighed and reluctantly shoved the plate back toward him. "You have to eat something."

He shrugged. "Yeah, those three already nibbled carrot sticks at nine in the morning sure look too tempting to pass up." And even though his voice dripped with sarcasm, he did eat them, and Gennie smiled again.

"OK," Pat announced when the last scrap was gone from Gennie's plate. "Let's go."

"Where?" she asked.

"To the races."

"What do you mean?"

"Let's go to the track."

"Why?"

"Because you need to go there."

She stopped cold. He knew her too well. "I'm OK, Pat, really. I was going to go back to Rob's and keep working on his tack room. The guys just let it go to hell—"

Rob saw what was happening and took the opportunity to announce that he was meeting the vet at the tack room, so cleaning would have to wait for another day. Gennie knew that Pat's intent stare meant there was no other option. She carried her plate to the cleanup area, waved goodbye to the cooks, and took Pat's outstretched hand.

They followed the crushed stone path from the kitchen through the barn area to the paddock, where horses were being walked to cool down from their late morning workouts. From there, the path continued under the grandstand and out to the track. The outriders, paramedics, and nearly everyone standing inside the rail nodded or said, "Hi," or, "Welcome back," to Gennie as she and Pat kept moving silently to the big oval. When the white rail did a ninety-degree turn to either side of them, they were left unguarded on the deep, soft dirt track with another white rail facing them across the way. Beyond that rail was the giant tote board listing the first race's roster and the morning odds. The clock was ticking down to post time. The rail in front of them had a skinny vertical board reading "Kensington Downs" so every winner's photo featured the track name. The finish line wire was over their heads. Gennie took it all in, looking up and down the track and turning around to see the stands slowly becoming populated with the day's audience. All the while, Pat held tight to her hand.

She smiled at him, pulled her hand away, and walked a few more yards past the wire. She focused her eyes on the dirt until she got to her destination. She saw Pat's boots as her eyes remained fixed on the ground. She knelt and picked up a handful of the freshly groomed dirt. "This is exactly where it happened," she said, letting the soil cascade from her cupped hand.

"I know."

"Do you think he's still here? I mean, I don't know …"

Pat knelt next to her and put his arm around her. "At our first race after the funeral, Ruben said that Hank's spirit would always be here since he died here. He said he could still feel him here."

Gennie looked at him quizzically. "Ruben said that? Was he drunk? Or was he messing with you?"

"No, I don't think so. He can be weird that way sometimes. I think he meant it. And when I thought about it, it made sense. It made me kinda feel good. I thought you'd like that thought, too. Hank's always here now, maybe watching over the rest of us."

She nodded as Pat took her hand to pull her back up to standing and continued, "Hundreds of other races have been run here since, and thousands more will. And you know Hank would understand that. And instead of thinking about what did happen here, you'll eventually start thinking of what is happening here now. It'll take a while, but it'll get easier. You'll never forget; it'll hit you when you least expect it, but eventually, it will get easier."

She shuffled her boots in the dirt, took a deep breath, and finally lifted her eyes up to the sunny blue sky. "It's a beautiful day for racing," she said, with a slight quiver in her voice.

"It is now," he said, smiling at her. "Are you going to be OK?" He squeezed her hand.

She met his concerned eyes. "Yes. I do want to be here. I feel like I'm with Hank by being here. Maybe he is here, and maybe he wanted me back."

"We all did," Pat said as he smiled, put a reassuring arm around her shoulder, and led her back to the barns. She wiped her eyes one last time and smiled.

Past Performances

"So, who was he?"

Pat and Gennie were sitting in the stands, watching the day's last race. A week had passed since her return, and already they'd developed a routine of hanging out for the day's last race if Pat wasn't riding. His arm was around Gennie's shoulder. He was done riding for the day but still wore his white shirt, riding pants, and boots. The weekday crowd had thinned to only a few dozen spectators among the thousands of seats. Gennie was reading the daily program.

"Who?" she asked, looking up to see what she had missed.

"The tall guy with a nice car." Pat kept his eyes on the track.

"What are you talking about?" she asked in confusion, still looking around.

Pat sighed. "During the school year, you were seen around town with a tall guy in a nice car. It doesn't matter, but I was just wondering who he was."

Her mouth fell open, and then she closed it tight. After a moment, she started again. "I was 'seen' around town? Were you following me?"

"No one was following you. It's just a small town."

"Sure is," she said and went back to her reading.

After a few more seconds Pat began again. "So?"

"Pat, you said it doesn't matter, so why even go there?"

"I guess I have to go there. It's been on my mind for months. Driving me crazy. You were supposed to be as miserable as me, not out and about around town with some tall guy in a nice car. The one time I see you in your fancy apartment, you're wearing a homecoming sweatshirt. I seem to recall that you usually go to homecoming with a date." His voice was emotional. Gennie couldn't tell if it was anger or distress.

She put the program on the empty seat on the other side of her and stayed quiet. She looked out to the vast track ahead like Pat was also doing. She took a deep breath and began. "I can't believe you noticed that stupid sweatshirt. I thought you were wasted."

Pat's eyes remained fixed on the track dirt. "I mean, of course, it makes sense. A hot new girl shows up for senior year. Of course, all the guys would flock to her."

Gennie closed her eyes tightly. "It wasn't like that at all. Don't be an idiot." She opened her eyes to watch the horses for the last race enter the starting gate. "He was just a guy from school. We hung out—mostly doing homework and going to school basketball games. His parents were going through a divorce, so we had a lot to talk about."

"So you talked a lot. And watched games." Pat's eyes didn't stray from the backstretch where the horses were in the gate, waiting for their release.

Gennie shrugged. "Yeah, I guess. Well, in all honesty, I watched the games. He played them."

The gate crashed open.

Pat flinched. "Jesus Christ. You're shitting me, right? He was a basketball player?"

She shrugged. "State Division 3. He was the forward. Not a big deal."

"You couldn't have befriended a baseball player, a track star, or even a football jerk? You had to go with basketball?"

"Cool down. It was nice having help changing lightbulbs for once." She finally grinned and snuck a sideways glance to see if he'd lighten up, but he remained stone-faced. She dropped the smile and bit her bottom lip.

They both were silent for a long time as they watched the horses coming for the home stretch. After they crossed the finish line, he spoke again. "Did you care for him?"

"Not in the way I care for you." She kept looking ahead, too.

"Good answer," he said quietly.

She saw out of the corner of her eye a slight smile on his face finally.

"Pat, I—"

"Maybe that is enough," he said.

"Didn't you—?" she began.

"I lived in utter misery and despair every minute you were gone," he said smugly with the same wicked grin. "I mean, of course, I had to fend Kelsey off with a stick several times."

"Fool," she said.

"Maybe."

She threaded her fingers into his hand resting over her shoulder and squeezed.

"You know I'm never letting you go again, right?" he asked, still looking ahead, still smiling, holding onto her hand tightly.

"You better not," she answered, smiling. They sat that way long after the crowd had left the stands, alone among the thousands of green seats, until the cleaning crew came through to clean up the abandoned copies of the *Racing Form* and the torn-up losing tickets.

***

On the anniversary of her father's death, the track named the feature race in his honor: the Harrison Mile. Gennie was asked to present the trophy to the owners of the winning horse, and she was thrilled when one of Rob's colts won with Pat aboard. Although no one said it out loud, many felt that Hank's spirit was there, guiding things along. Ruben remained silent but smiled at Gennie, kissed his index finger, and pointed to the sky. There were more tears than cheers in the winner's circle when Rob insisted that Gennie keep the trophy for herself. Nearly every rider came to her that day with colorful stories about Hank. The rider who had been hurt in the same spill even gave her a bouquet of carnations. It was a bittersweet day, remembering how much had changed in those two minutes. Looking back, Gennie could hardly believe that only twelve months had passed.

***

Gennie saw Ray once that summer. She was in the paddock before a race, holding onto one of Rob's more frisky colts as he got the saddle cinch tightened. She kept talking to the colt and trying to distract him from the excitement going on around him. The outside paddock stall was closest to the public walkway where spectators could come to view the next race's entries. Standing there, she heard muffled voices and her name among the words they said. She looked over her shoulder to see Ray and a bunch of his buddies at the rail, smoking cigars, holding programs, and staring at her. She quickly realized that it was Ray's birthday, and this must be his guys' day out. They waved at her, and she just smiled while holding the colt's bridle with both hands. He started getting more nervous and doing some high-step prancing while Rob explained the strategy to use in the upcoming race to the jockey. Gennie spoke softly to the colt until he focused on her and calmed down enough that Rob could lift the rider into the stirrups. Gennie then released the lead rope to the pony rider and headed to the rail where the guys still waited. She realized she was glad she had washed her hair after the morning workouts and that Pat had been the first rider to leave the paddock.

"So this is your summer job?" Ray said in faked amazement, waving his arms to emphasize the whole place.

She shrugged and smiled. "Yep." She nodded in greeting to the rest of the guys.

"Does it pay good?" one of the others asked.

"Nope," she said.

"Are you a jockey, too?" another asked.

"Nope," she answered.

"Looks dangerous," Ray said. "That horse could have stomped you."

Gennie shrugged. "That's my job to make sure he doesn't stomp me or anyone else around him. He was just showing off a bit to impress the rest of the field."

"Can you give us a good tip for this race?" asked one of the friends.

"Yep, number seven, that horse I was with. Today's his day. He's psyched."

"Cool," the guy answered and scurried to get to the betting windows. The other guys, except Ray, followed, still looking at their programs and tripping over each other.

"You surprised?" she asked Ray, who was looking down at her muck-filled boots.

"Nah, I knew you worked here. That's why I suggested we come here. It's my birthday."

"I know. Sorry, I forgot. Happy birthday! But how did you know I worked here?"

227

"Anita told me your dad was a jockey, so I guessed, but then I called your mom to ask her before she left."

"You called my mom?" she asked, taken aback.

"I was just curious, that's all. You were so mysterious and everything. I figured you either worked at the racetrack or were an exotic dancer or something."

She laughed and shook her head. "Sorry to disappoint. I know you've been holding onto that exotic dancer dream."

He looked serious. "Is it working out here? The job, I mean."

"Yeah, I live in my own place, which is cool. And my cousin's the starter—the guy who controls the starting gate—so it's good to be around family again. Really, everyone who works here is like one big family. It's great."

Ray nodded. "Yeah, it seems exciting." Gennie noticed that he seemed melancholy.

"How about you? Are you and Susan still together?" she asked, sincerely interested.

He smiled shyly and shook his head. "She was driving me nuts. I told her I needed some space, some time off before going to school, to figure myself out."

Gennie smiled sympathetically, nodding in understanding. "I know what you mean. Hey, I have to get out there to see the race. I'll meet you by the rail, OK?" she said, noticing that he seemed to brighten with the suggestion. She rushed down the dirt path to where the trainers and other grooms usually gathered to watch the race just outside the winner's circle. Rob was looking through his binoculars to watch the horses enter the starting gate.

"Who was that?" he asked as Gennie came up next to him.

"Who?" she asked, straining to look where he was looking.

"That guy in the paddock?"

228

"Oh, geez," she said, relaxing. "He's from high school. My own personal stalker."

"He looks like a nice young man," Rob said, still gazing through the glasses.

"He is a very nice young man," she agreed.

"Hmm."

"And I'll see you in the winner's circle after the race, OK?" she said.

"I like your optimism," Rob said, still watching the horses load into the starting gate through his binoculars.

She slipped under the guardrail to the public side, where the guys were assembled along the rail, holding their tickets and programs and watching the clock countdown to post time.

"I hope you're right," one of them said, "because I bet the whole bootie kitty on number seven."

"I hope I am, too, because grooms get a portion of the purse if they win," she said with a smile, finding herself excited to be with a group of novices in an arena she was familiar with. "Have you ever been to the races?" she asked Ray.

"Once with my dad a few years ago," he said. "All I remember is that he won one really big bet, and we went out to a fancy dinner."

The bells clashed, and the race began. It was a six-furlong sprint for maidens—horses that had never won a race. Gennie leaned on the rail with anticipation as she watched for the red-and-black silks to come around the corner. As they entered the stretch, the rider had the colt alongside the rail just behind the two leaders. "That's good, that's good," Gennie reassured her old friends. The rider was saving the colt's energy, and as they approached the tote board, he had to use only one tap of the whip to urge the colt forward to win by a length. Despite herself,

Gennie jumped in the air and gave the thumbs-up sign to Rob across the way.

Ray's friends were hooting and high-fiving as they lit up more cigars. Gennie excused herself to go to her winner's circle duties, but Ray's friend grabbed her wrist. "Dinner's on me," he said, "for everyone after the last race. You in?"

She smiled genuinely at their excitement. "Yeah, count me in. Sounds fun. I'll meet you here after the ninth." She went to the winner's circle to hold the lead rope for the traditional winner's photo. She rubbed the colt's nose and planted a kiss on him. The colt raised his head and looked at her for more praise. She congratulated the rider and started to lead the horse back to the barns. Pat, who had ridden the second-place horse, was ahead as she started back. She walked quickly and saw Ray out of the corner of her eye, still watching her. She ignored him and tried to catch up to Pat.

"Hey," she called, and he turned around.

"Darn that colt," he said, stopping to rub its neck. "I almost had him."

"Shush, now I can pay for a movie on Saturday," she said. "Hey, I ran into some old friends, and they invited me to dinner tonight, so I'm not going to be at the diner, OK?"

He seemed surprised. "Old friends? You don't have old friends." He didn't say it cruelly, only factually.

"Old as in last year. From school. They're here gambling and smoking cigars, and I gave them a good tip, so they want to pay me back."

"Sure, fine, have fun," he said, surprised that she even asked.

She wondered why she didn't tell Pat it was the tall guy with a nice car. He would have expected her to tell him it was. But she didn't—couldn't. She told herself they were talking in such a noisy setting that it would have been too complicated to explain. It was just easier not to mention it, she rationalized.

For those watching Pat, they might have seen his eyes dart behind Gennie to scan the crowd for who she might be referring to. But that was it. He was fine.

After Gennie walked the winning colt around the cool-down circle for a while, she put him back in his stall with some treats for his excellent performance and then grabbed a clean pullover from the backpack she kept in the tack room. But there was nothing she could do about her jeans and boots. Even though no one was there to see her, she shrugged and said, "What you see is what you get."

The dinner was fun for her. They went back to O'Casey's for old times' sake and talked about their day's conquests and defeats, and they all listened with great interest to Gennie's analysis of the day's races and how the mistakes they made could have been avoided. "If Rob Wayne ever has a two-year-old entered in its first race, bet on it. He never races a two-year-old unless he's sure that they can win. It's his specialty," she said. One of the guys even took notes. They discussed coming back on Saturday now that they had a system in place, and maybe Gennie could meet them earlier in the day and help them with their picks. She laughed.

"Today was your beginner's luck day. If you want ongoing advice, it might cost you," she said, laughing, even though one of the guys offered to pay her for more tips. She just shook her head and laughed. "Not gonna happen. Sorry, dude."

Ray remained quiet for most of the dinner. "You OK?" she asked.

He seemed surprised. "Oh, yeah, sure. It's just weird being back here. The kids suddenly look so young," he said, nodding toward other tables of students from St. Joe's. "Life is already so different." She nodded in agreement.

He looked at her again. "You know, when I first saw you at Joe's, I thought you looked familiar. Now that I realize how close this is to the track, I bet I saw you here before you started school."

Gennie smiled. "Well, I guess that could be true. I did come here occasionally and was usually intimidated by all the pretty and affluent students staring me down."

"Hmm."

After dinner, they drove her all the way back to Rob's farm. Gennie apologized profusely for forgetting about the long drive home when she accepted their offer, but the guys all agreed it was a nice night for a scenic drive … in the dark. As they pulled onto Rob's gravel driveway, she thanked them all multiple times for the fun evening and the ride home.

When she got out of the car, Ray followed her. "Walking me to the door?" she asked.

"Sure, for old times' sake," he replied. "This place looks like it might be dangerous. Treacherous sorts hanging about. I wouldn't want you to get hurt." He made a point of looking carefully around the moonlit well-manicured front yard leading to the recently painted stables.

"Ray, it was good to see you," she said, smiling.

"It was good seeing you. You look great. Really. And happy."

"I am happy," she said, turning to him as she reached her door.

"So are you seeing someone?" he asked while looking casually around the stable area, avoiding her eyes as they stood under her doorway porch light.

"Yeah, I am," she answered with a tight-lipped smile.

"Figured. Mystery Man, right?"

"I'm sorry, Ray. I probably should have never gotten involved with you. I had no idea—" She took his hands and squeezed them.

He smiled down at her and squeezed her hands back. "No, no, I'm glad you did. Now I know how it should feel."

"OK, now stop. I don't need a guilt trip." She pulled away and turned to put her key in the lock to break his gaze.

"No guilt, but just one more thing," he said, trying to get her attention back. "Why such a big secret about working in horse racing? What's the big deal?" he asked, waving his hand toward the stable yard.

She shrugged. "I guess the bigger thing was having dropped out for a year. That just seemed so anti-private-school girl. I just—I don't know. I just wanted a fresh start—no prejudices against the poor dropout with muck on her boots. And I needed to get away from it. After my dad died, it was ... it was just hard to be there anymore. I didn't want to be part of racing anymore."

"I think you underestimated us, or at least me."

"I guess I felt I couldn't take that chance. What was the point? It shouldn't have mattered to anyone."

"I just—I don't know. I guess I don't understand why you never talked about it to me, or Anita even. Did you not trust us?"

Gennie thought about it, her eyes looking down at the gravel. "It wasn't that I didn't trust you. I just didn't want you to know. I wanted you to be part of my new life, and I wanted to leave the old behind. If I kept talking about it, I wouldn't move on."

"But you obviously didn't want to move on."

She sighed. "Got me there. But I wasn't sure. I thought I wanted to. I wanted to want to. We're back to that. I shouldn't have ever gotten involved with you. It wasn't fair when I was so messed up inside. I'm sorry."

"Stop saying that. I had a great year."

She finally looked up and smiled at him. "I did, too. I really did. Better than I would have ever imagined. Happy birthday, Ray."

"It was," he said, kissing her quickly before she could protest. And surprisingly, she didn't. He released his lips but kept resting his forehead on hers. "Maybe I could send the guys home, and we could get caught up for a while."

She found herself not wanting to move away. "But then you wouldn't have a way to get home," she said softly.

"Darn," he whispered, with his breath sending that familiar shiver back down her spine.

She finally mustered up the courage to gently push him back. "Ray, don't tell anyone I said this, but if I could have two parallel lives, I would—but I can't. I'm sorry."

He gave a tight-lipped grin, then sighed, but noticed something shining on her neck. He gently pushed at her shirt's neckline to reveal the horseshoe pendant he had given her for Christmas. "You still wear it?" he asked, surprised.

She grinned sheepishly and shrugged. "I never take it off."

He was just about to speak when two loud honks pierced the evening air.

"DUDE! Come on!" one of his friends shouted from the car. Gennie and Ray both jumped and laughed. A horse from inside the barn whinnied loudly.

"OK, I think it's time for you to go home before you cause a stampede and wake up my landlords," Gennie said, pushing him toward the car. He held his hands up in defeat, made a dramatic bow to her, then turned and walked back to his friends.

"Maybe we'll see you in the winner's circle someday again," he called out without turning around.

"Maybe," she said, then added under her breath, "but it's a long shot." She waved under the stable light as they pulled out of the driveway.

Home Stretch

And so our heroine found her footing back on her home turf after her momentary detour into the life of an average teen. Her days returned to rising before the sun. Her hands regained their callouses. And her heart was given back to the track, her horses, and her favorite jockey. Well, her favorite living jockey.

Just when she thought she was settling into the life laid out for her, a new scene found her back in the track diner where the president of Kensington Downs, Mr. Michael Jenkins, joined her for breakfast. "Gennie, we're looking for a new office assistant to help our marketing and sales directors out. Would you be interested?"

Gennie was mid-sip of her black coffee. Her eyes widened, and she appeared unable to finish her swallow. Jenkins even leaned back in case she was about to spit it out. She looked down at the table for a few seconds, breathed in through her nose, and finally swallowed. "Um, what exactly does an office assistant do?" she asked, finally looking back up.

He smiled back. "Oh, nothing too fancy. Mostly clerical. Making copies, paying invoices, booking ads with the local TV and radio stations … whatever the team needs help with. It's a small crew, so I reckon you'd start helping out with events and such, too, like 'Meet the Jockeys Day' for kids. We normally require a college degree even for this role but, Gennie, we all know you and know you're more than capable of it. In fact, Kensington started a scholarship program a few years back for employees to continue their education. You could apply for that and take night classes in the fall. The only catch is that you have to commit to working at Kensington for two years after you get your degree." He flashed another warm smile and winked. Gennie thought for a moment that his face transformed into Hank's when he gave that wink. She shuddered and held back a sudden rush of emotion. She found herself smiling, nodding, and shaking his hand.

She went to Rob's barn, where she found him finishing up with the farrier. "Hey, Rob, I don't suppose you had anything to do with Mr. Jenkins offering me a job in the office, did you?"

"What?" he asked. "Why would I do that if it means losing my favorite employee?" His smile told her all she needed to know.

"Thank you, Rob."

"But wait, does that mean you won't want to be grooming at 4:00 a.m. anymore?" Rob asked morosely.

She wasn't sure if he was serious or not. "I could, if you need me to, but only until 8:00 a.m. because that's when Mr. Jenkins said I'd need to be in the office."

Rob laughed and shook her hand. "Congratulations, Gennie. You've taken your first real job, and it pays a helluva lot better than I do. If I see you around my stables stealing secrets, I'll shush you away." Gennie jumped up, gave him a big hug, and then rushed back to the jocks' room to tell Pat. She had to wait until he finished a ping-pong game with one of the new apprentice riders, beating him handily, of course.

As soon as he walked over, she told him everything about the job in one breath, briefly exhaled, and then continued. "And I told Rob I'd still take care of some horses just because I want to."

Pat smiled. "This is really great. Everything's falling into place," he said, "especially if you take night classes in the fall—hell, I might even take them with you."

Gennie's eyes lit up. "Would you? Oh my God, that would be great. Can you imagine us doing homework together?" She giggled like a schoolgirl.

He sat on the bench next to her and turned to study her smiling face. "Don't get scared by this," he said. "I'm just thinking out loud."

Her smile disappeared; her eyes widened. She was nervous. What had she not thought of? Was he mad that she hadn't talked to him first? Did he want her to stay in the stables? She expected terrible news. He was switching tracks, he was gaining weight, or he was dying of an incurable disease. She should have known better than to get hopeful.

"With this new job of yours, and if I keep going at the pace I'm going … if we each start setting aside a couple of bucks each week, we could seriously buy a horse or two next year."

Her eyes widened at the unsuspected suggestion. "Rob said I could still stay there rent free if I took care of his horses out there, so, hell, yeah, I could bank most everything I earn. And with Kensington paying for school …" her voice drifted off into her rapidly spinning head full of ideas.

"… We could even afford a wedding in there, sometime, I mean, not right away, but—" she heard distantly in her daze.

"Wait, what?" she asked, suddenly sitting up straight, eyes even wider, a smile creeping back.

"Well, I said I didn't want to scare you off, but I'm not going into business with someone who's not serious … I mean, not serious about everything," he explained, stumbling over the words and shrugging, suddenly looking down at the well-worn floor.

"Oh my God," she said, looking around the old familiar rec room: the exercise bikes, the scattered *Racing Forms*, the ping-pong table. "What is happening?" She avoided looking at Pat so he wouldn't see the tears welling up in her eyes. "Last year I was so mad … so mad … at this place that I never wanted to see it again. I really can't believe I'm back. Such a long shot …"

Pat smiled. "Long shots have the biggest payoffs."

She finally looked at him and smiled, forcing a few tears to find their way down her cheeks. Pat gently wiped them away.

"Do you realize this could be the best day of my life?" she asked.

"Then why are you crying?" he asked.

"I don't know. It's all just coming together, finally. I never thought there could be a happy ending, you know? But maybe everything does happen for a reason—even the shitty stuff. I don't know. It's complicated, isn't it?" Her smile returned in full, perhaps even with a little Hank twinkle in her eyes. She wiped away the last tears and looked at Pat to say, "But, note to yourself, that was not a proper proposal. I expect something better than that—I mean, not right away, but …"

"I promise I'll do better next time." Pat just grinned at her.

Gennie leaned back on the bench, smiling from ear to ear. Our camera zooms out from her content smile, revealing the cluttered rec room and rising above the track buildings, overlooking the whole of Kensington Downs where it all started and where it now ends—or is it just beginning?

***

Ray heard about the engagement just a year after college graduation. He and Anita kept in touch through occasional emails. She wrote that there was no date planned yet, but she had never seen Gennie so animated as when she bumped into her at O'Casey's during Christmas break. She told him that Gennie's mother and grandfather were investing in Gennie and Pat's dream of owning and training racehorses.

Ray had to drop out of basketball freshman year with a knee injury, but he graduated with a degree in engineering and quickly secured a job with an aeronautics firm in New York. Two years later, he married a girl whom he'd met, oddly enough, at Saratoga Race Course. He thought that the fact they had met there must be a sign of some sort because he fell in love quickly and deeply with her.

His wedding present to his bride was a share in a racehorse syndicate, which everyone assumed was just a sentimental homage to the way they had met. Anita was the only one who thought differently. She knew that Ray, even if he didn't admit it to himself, just wanted to keep up his chances of running into Gennie again one day at a racetrack where they might both happen to have horses running.

Anita graduated with a double major in journalism and film and moved to L.A. to see if she could make the big time out there. She also has a happy ending, having sold her first of many screenplays before she was twenty-five. Interestingly, the first one told a story remarkably similar to this one.

About the Author

Trish Dulka was born and raised in Milwaukee, WI. As a young girl, she developed a love for horses. As an older girl, she developed a love for romantic stories. *Chances Are* is her first novel. When not reading, listening to music, or helping on her sister's farm, you can find Trish hanging out with her husband, two kids, and their white Westie named Willoughby.

Printed in Great Britain
by Amazon

24102790R00138